THE OFFICIAL ONE PIECE STICKER BOOK

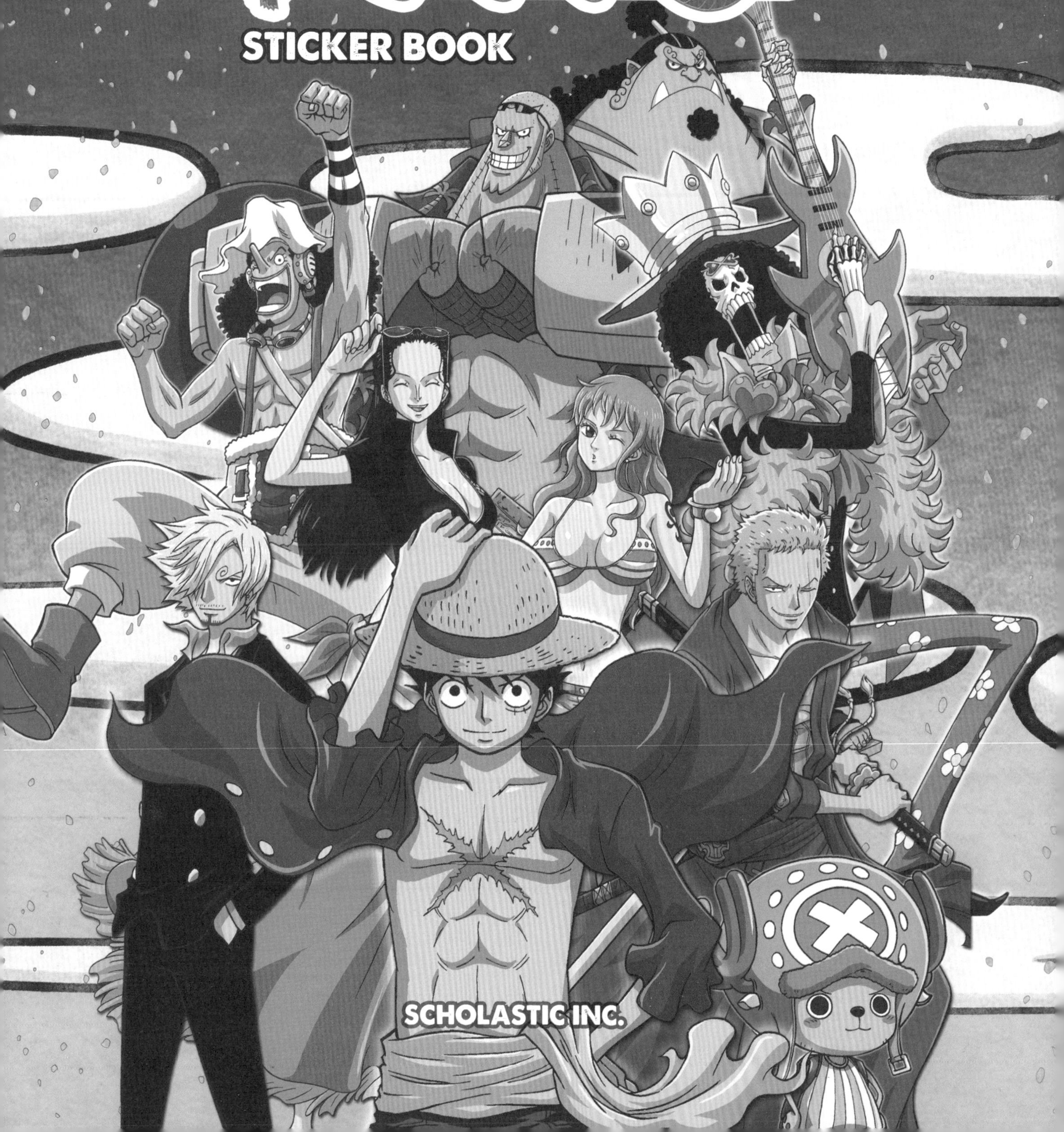

SCHOLASTIC INC.

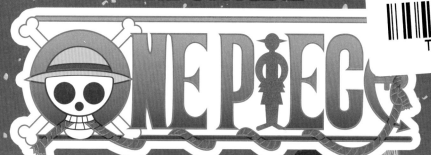

ISBN: 978-1-5461-3892-1

10 9 8 7 6 5 4 3 2 1   24 25 26 27 28

Printed in China
First printing 2024

Book design by Elliane Mellet
Art Direction by Salena Mahina

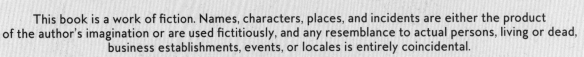

HOIST YOUR FLAG AND GET READY TO SET SAIL FOR THE GRAND LINE!

With more than 1,000 stickers, you can create your very own One Piece adventure with all your favorite characters, Devil Fruits, Den Den Mushi, and more! Apply these stickers to scenes in this book or add some pirate flair to anything you own—the choice is yours!

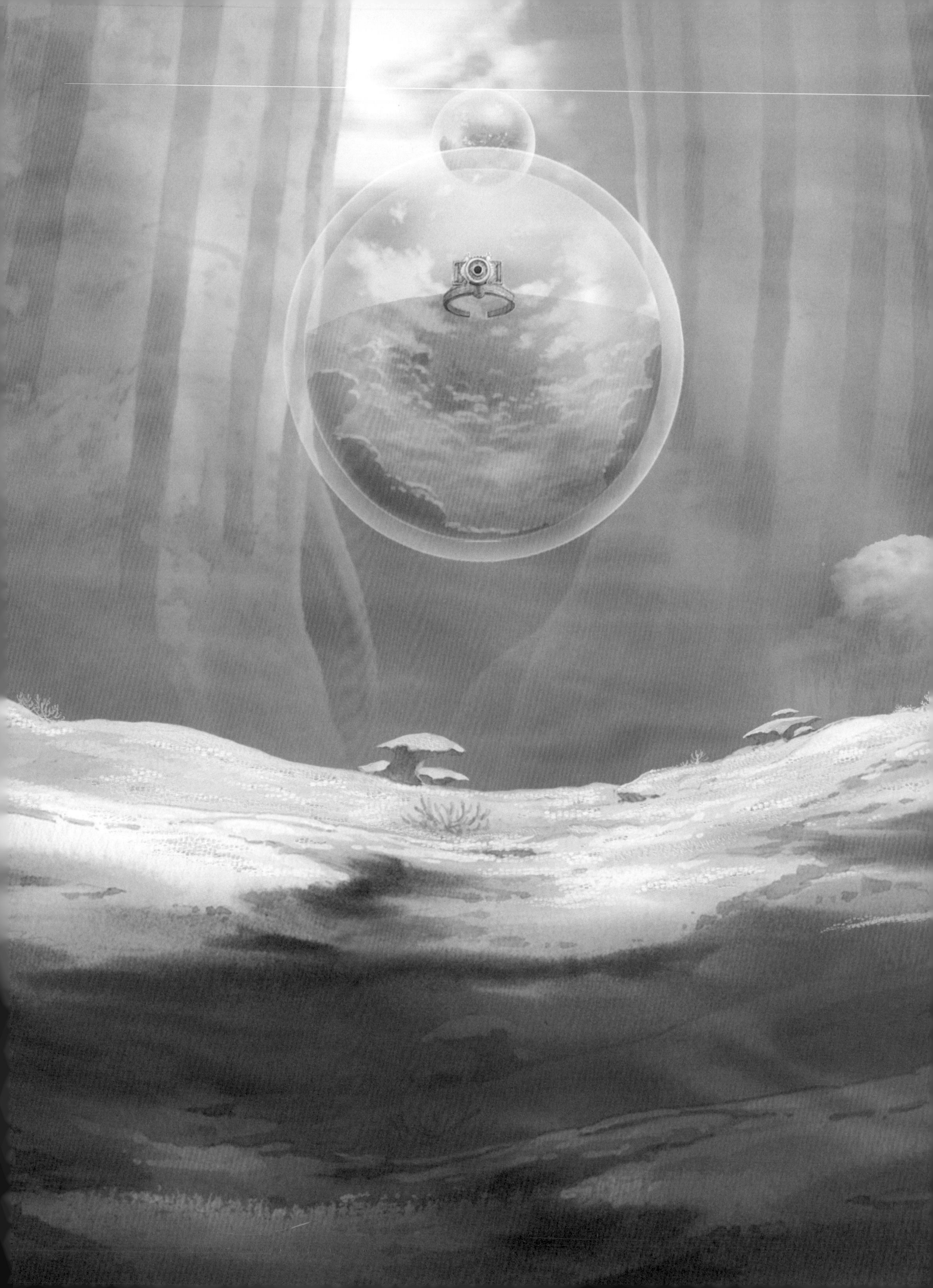

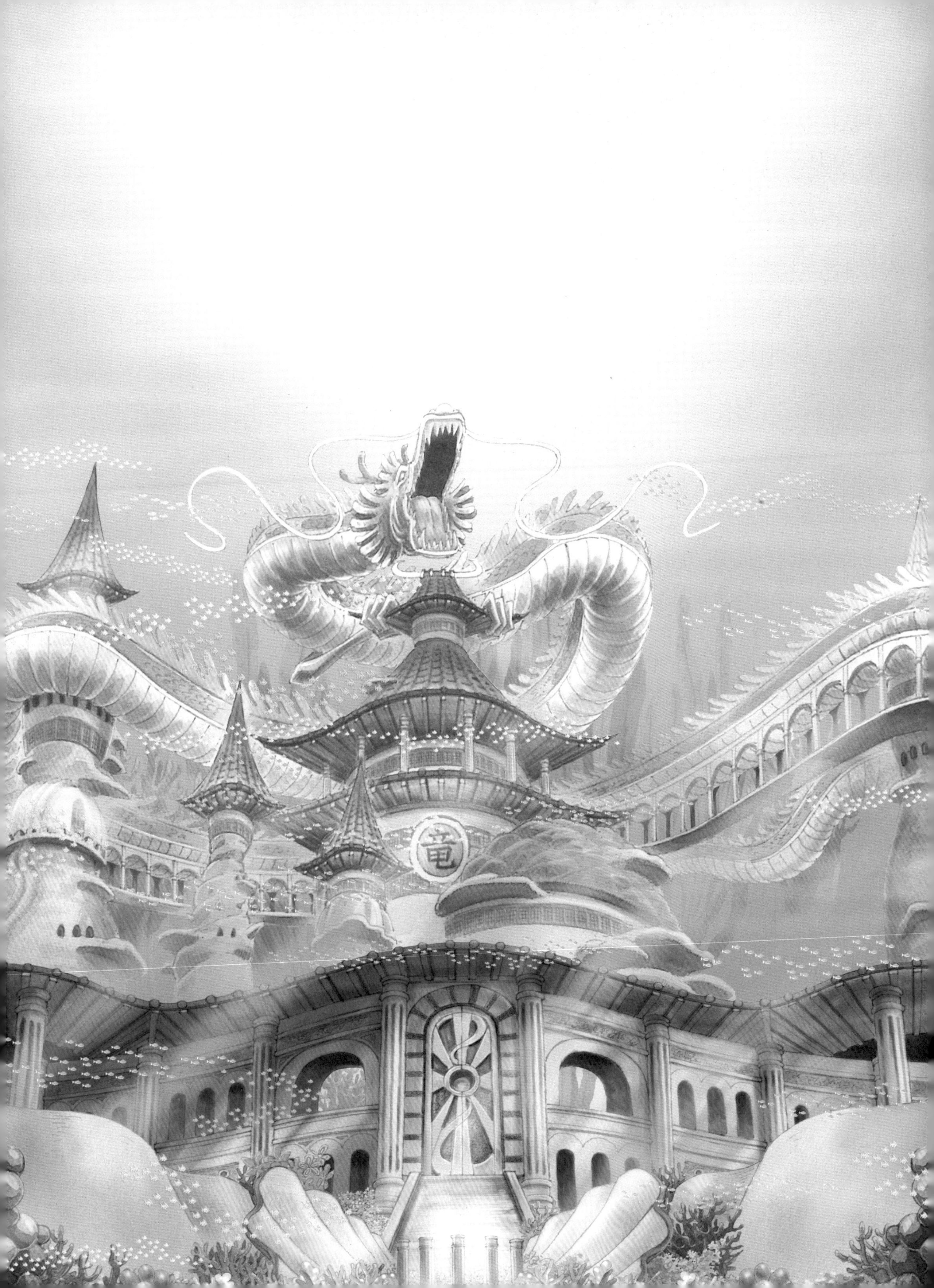
竜

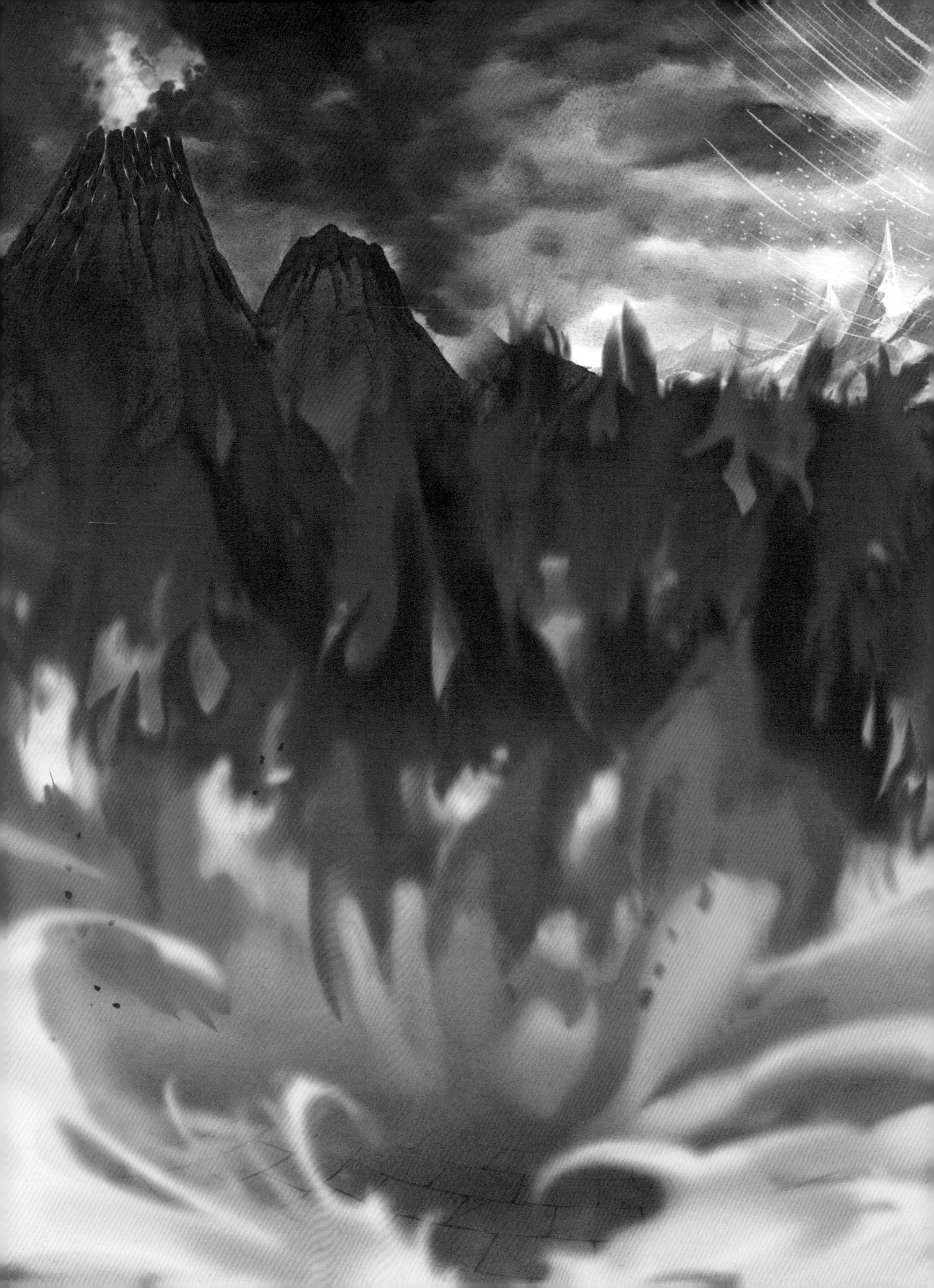

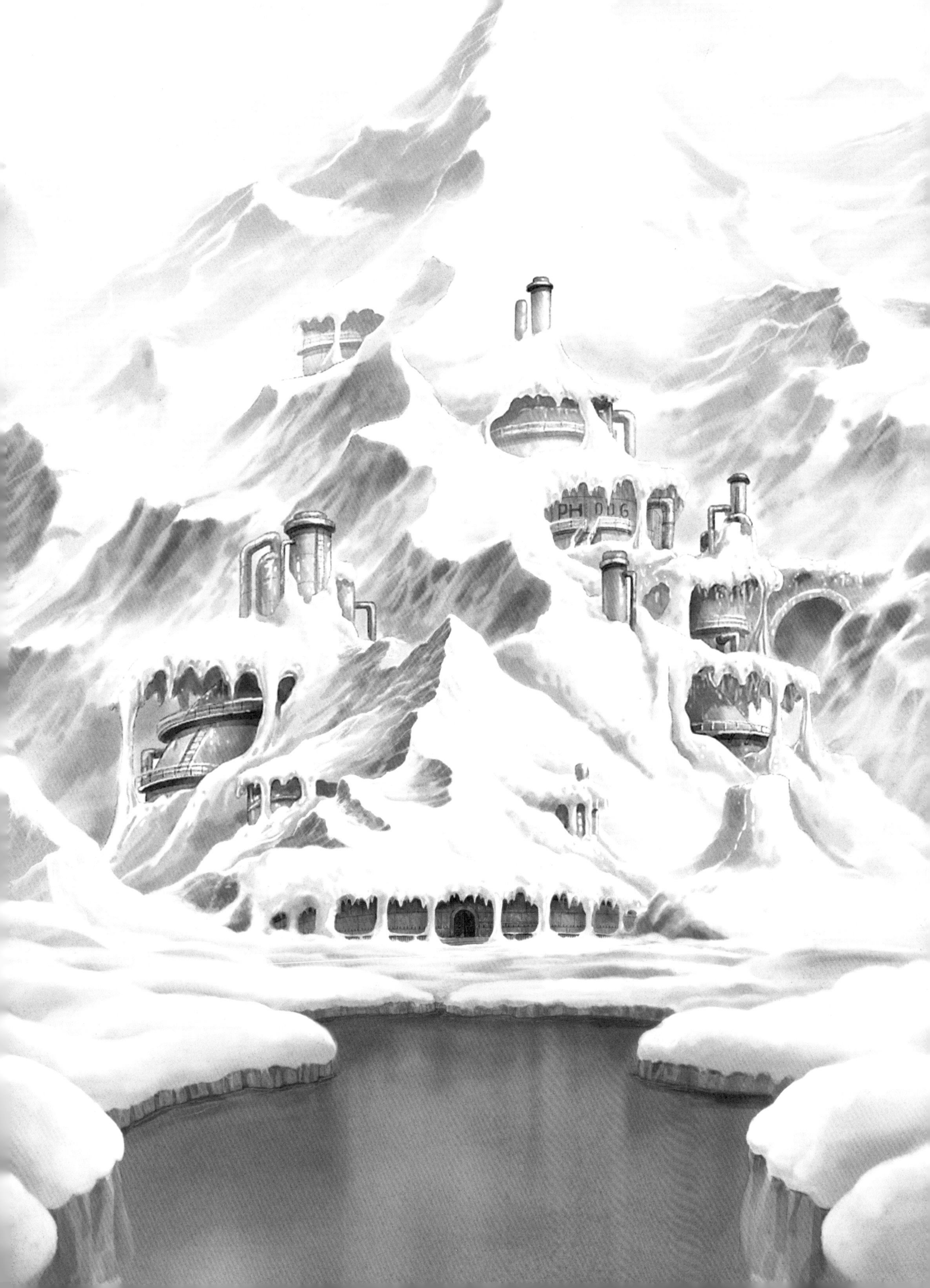
PH 006

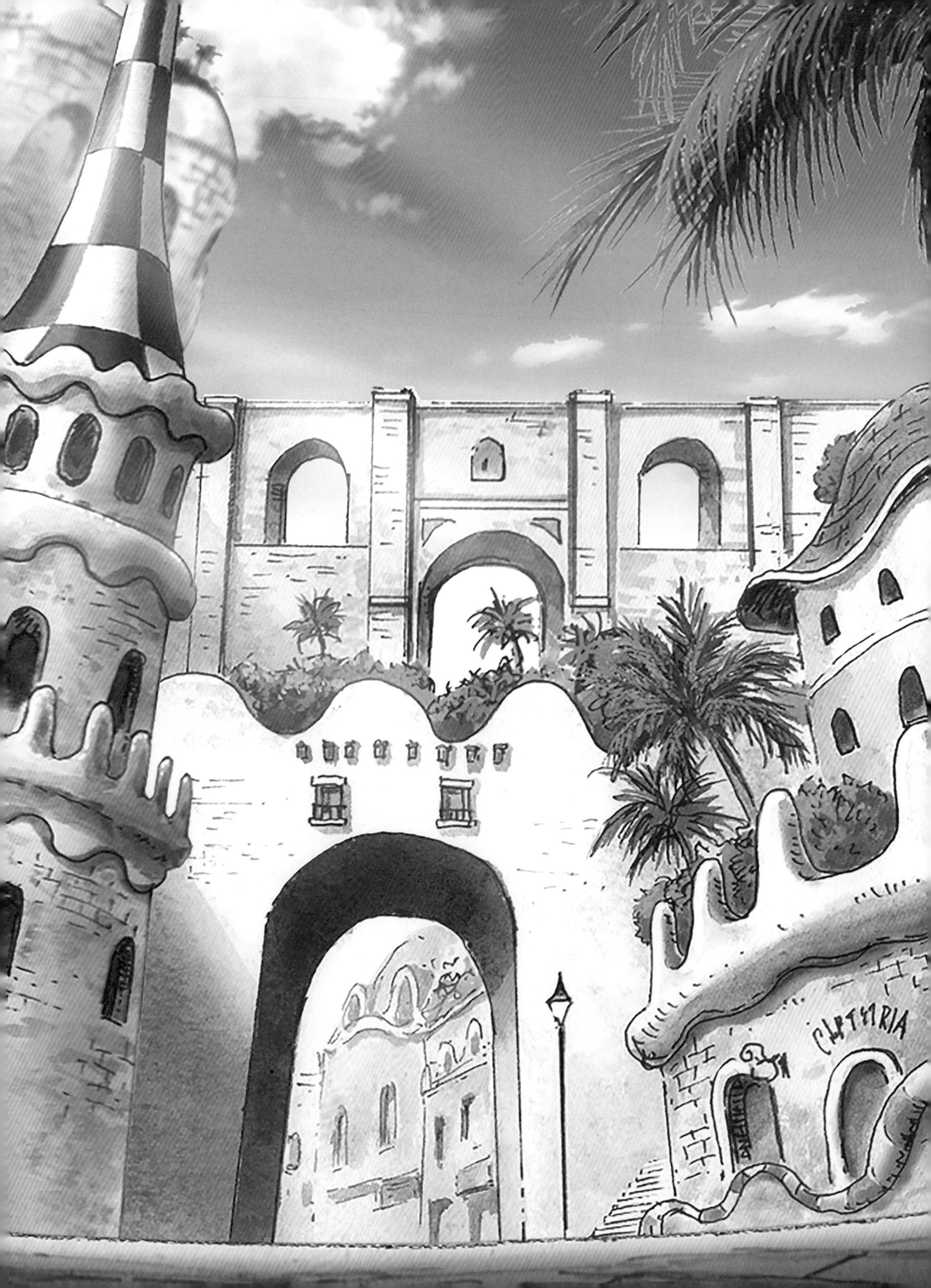

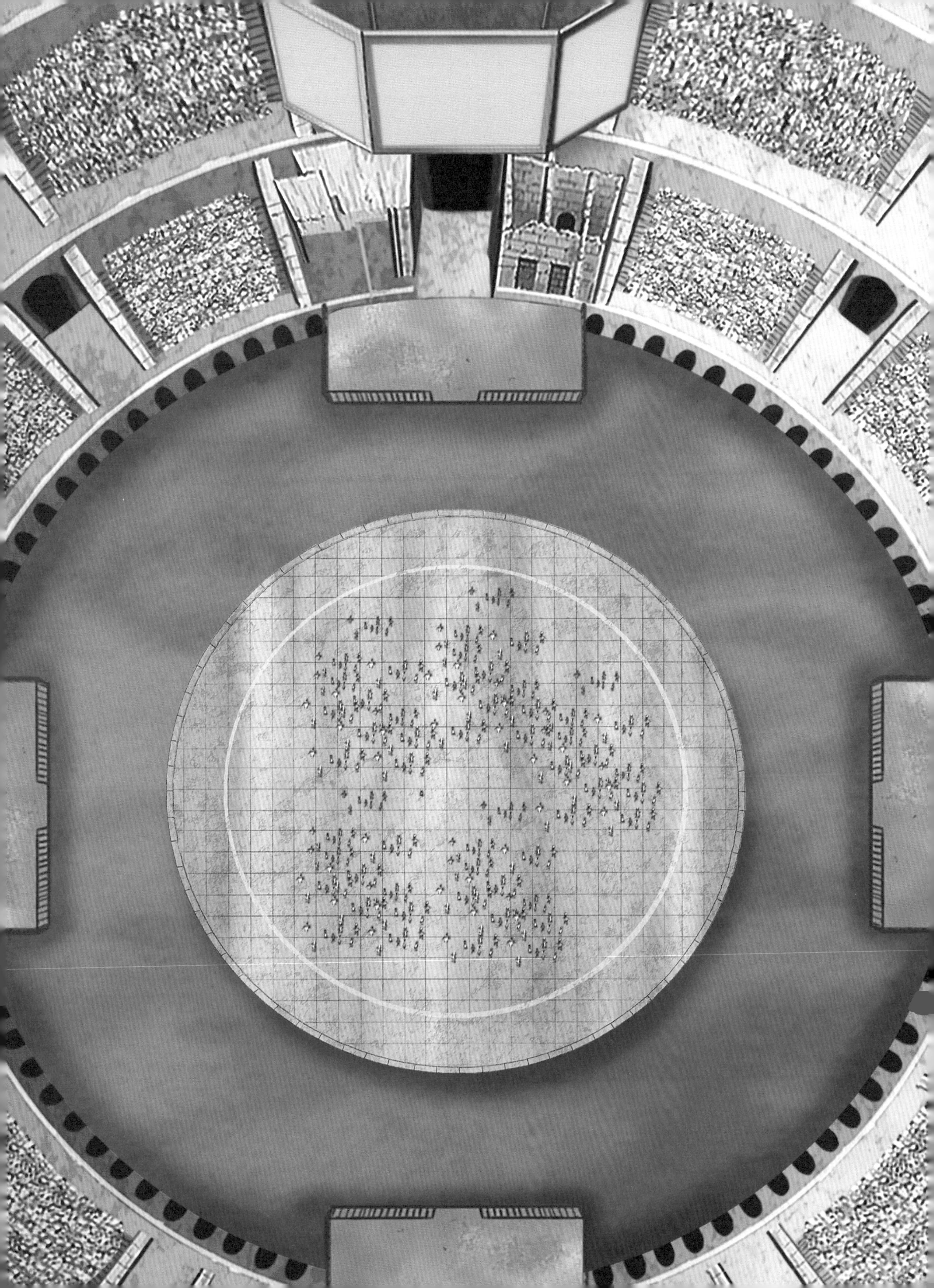

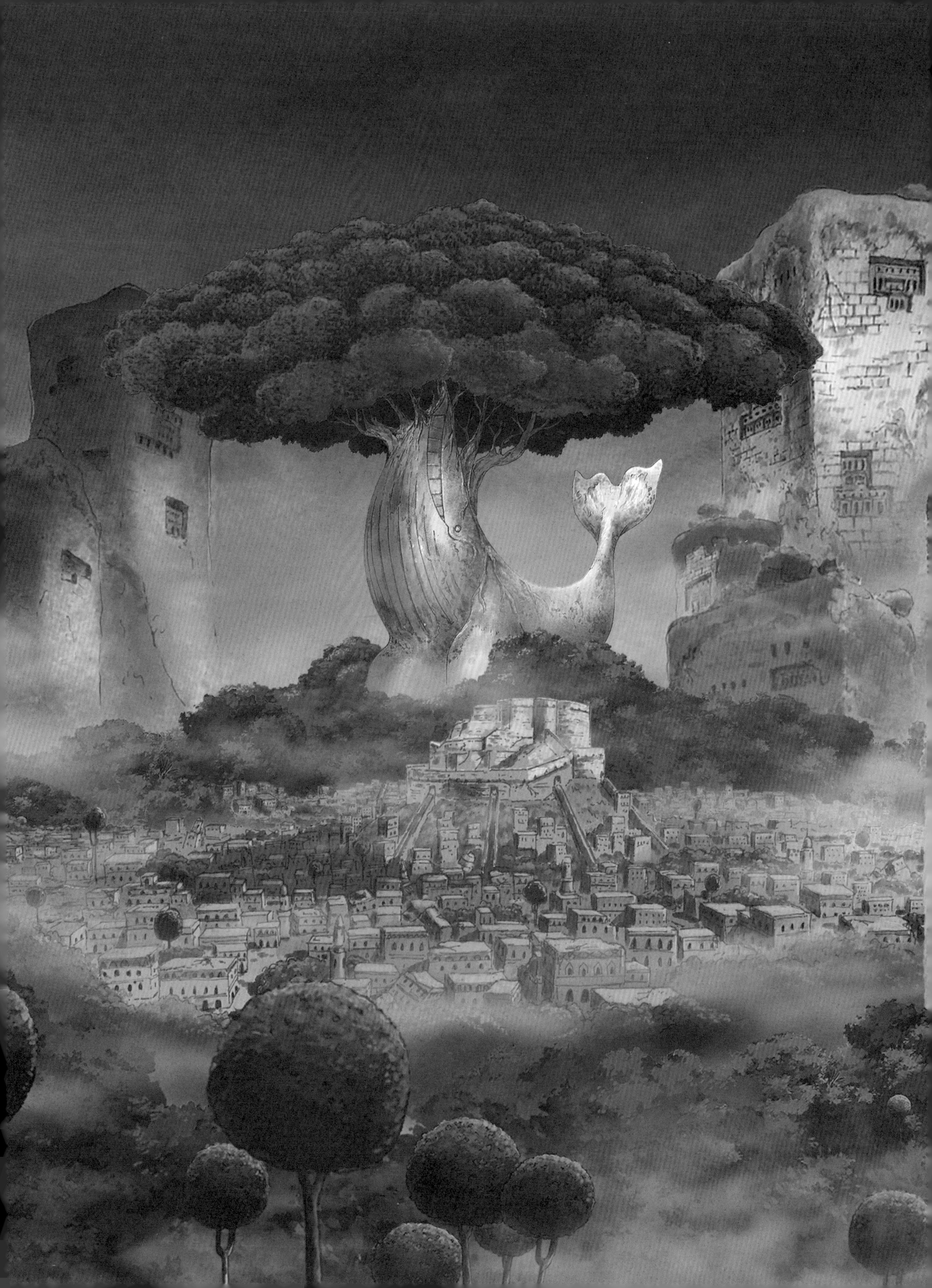

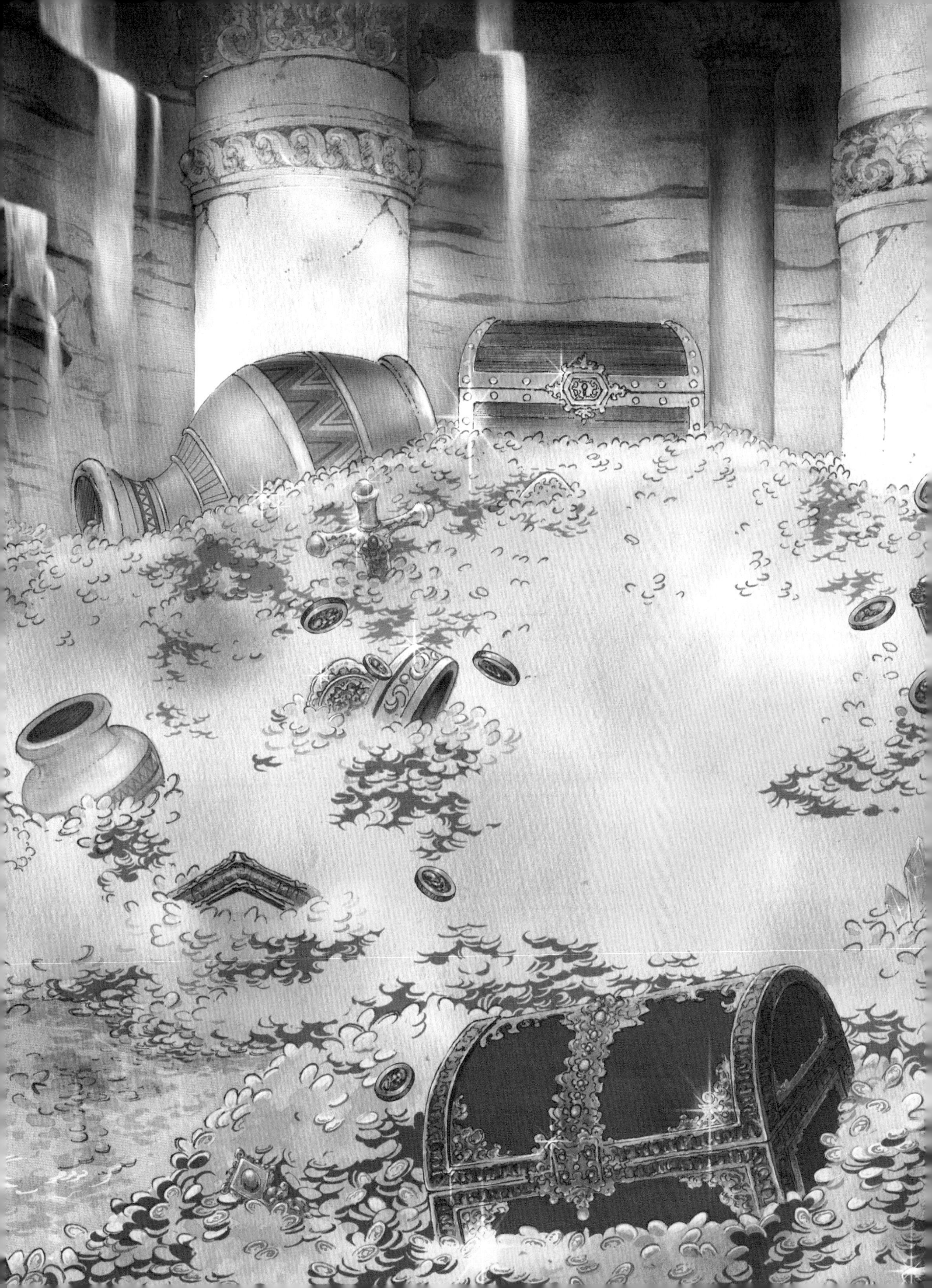

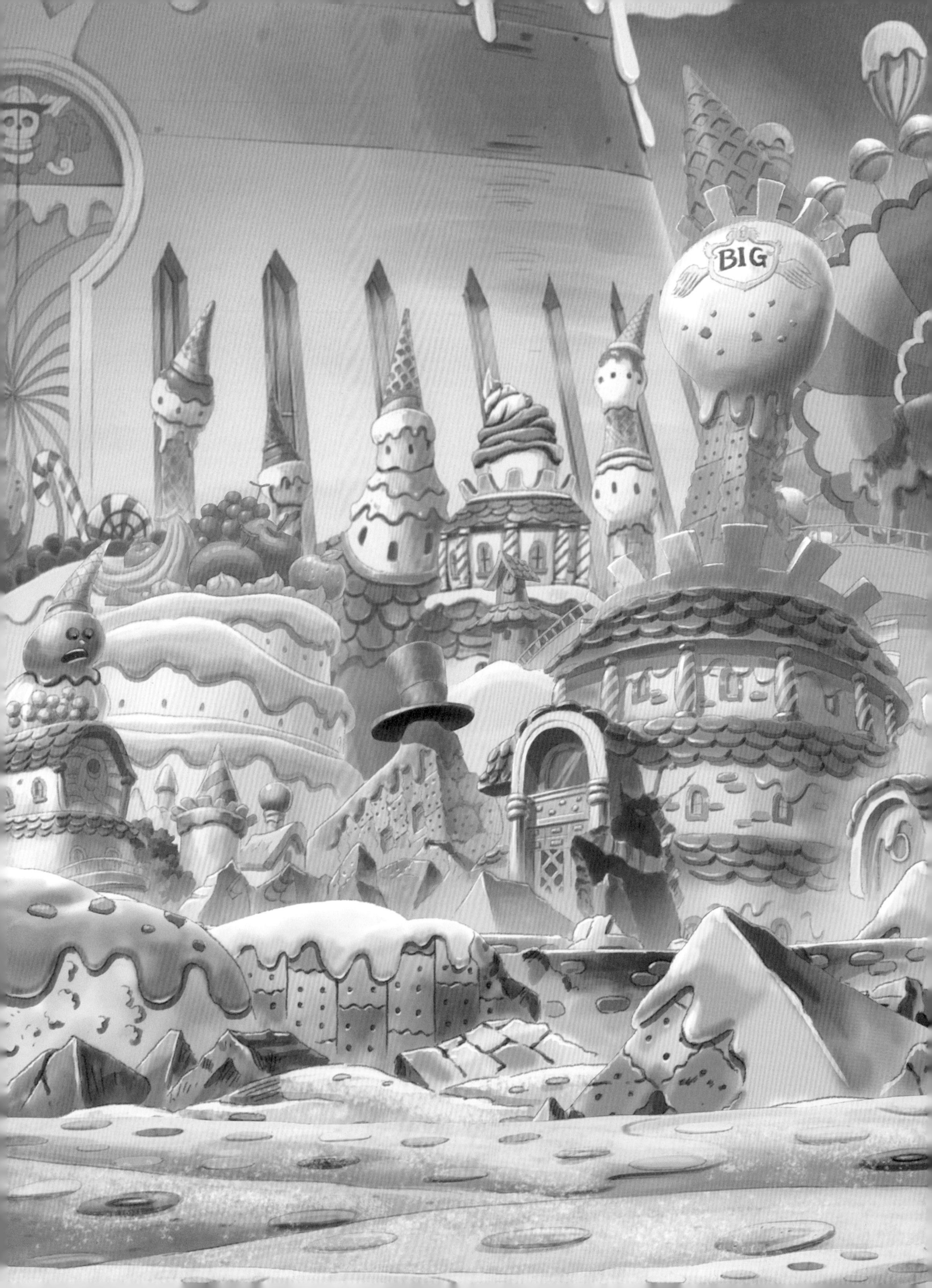
BIG

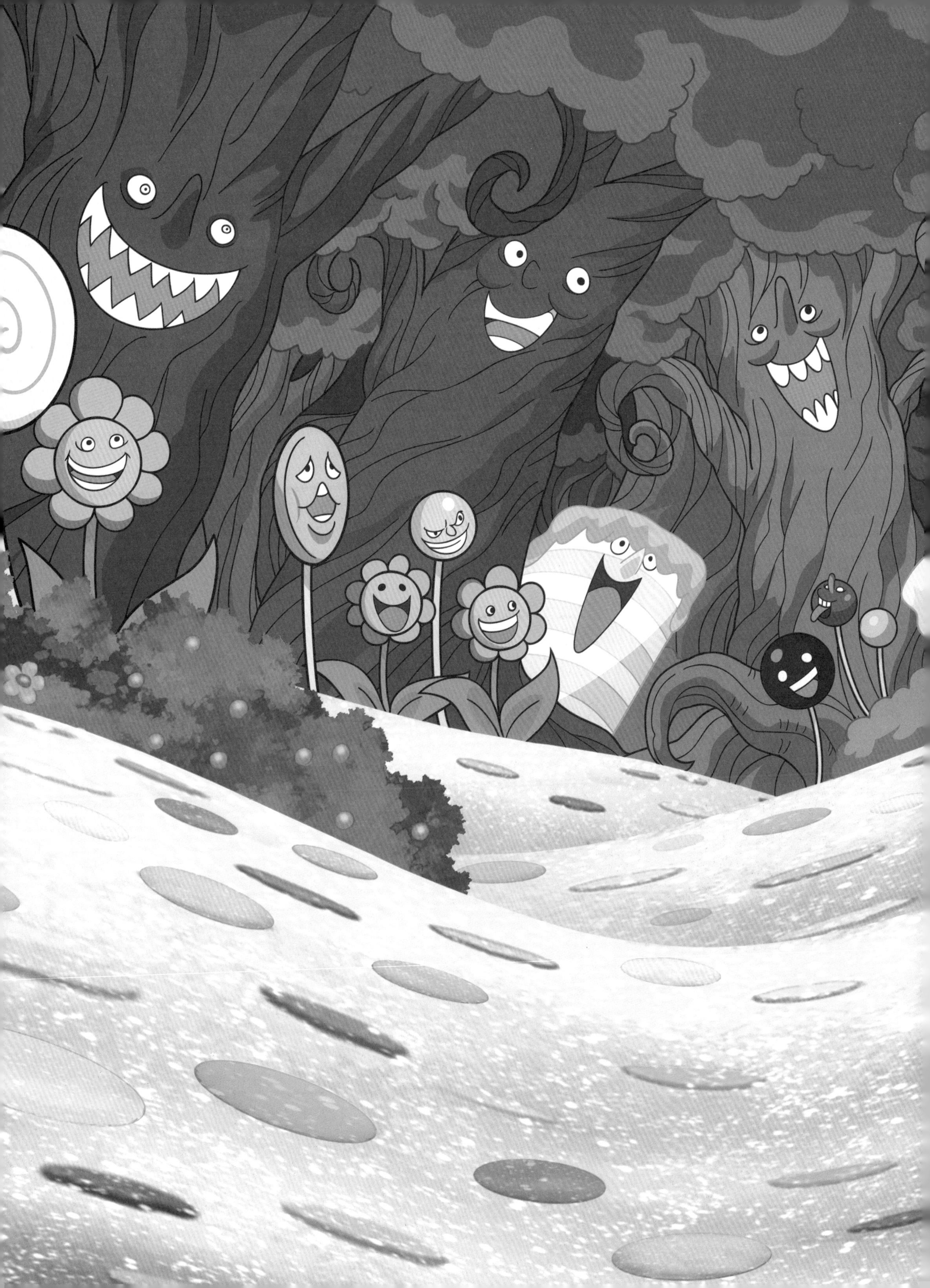

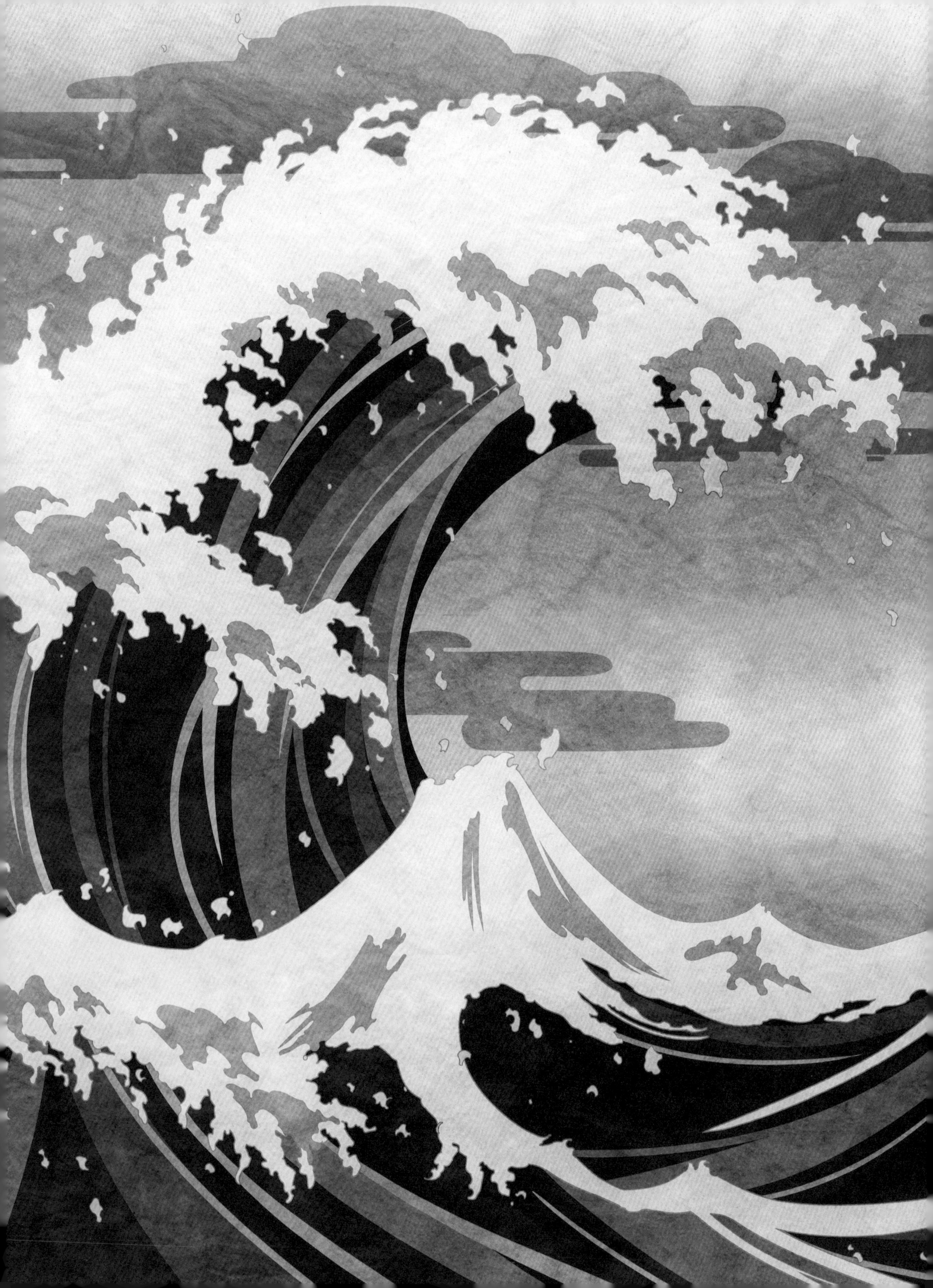

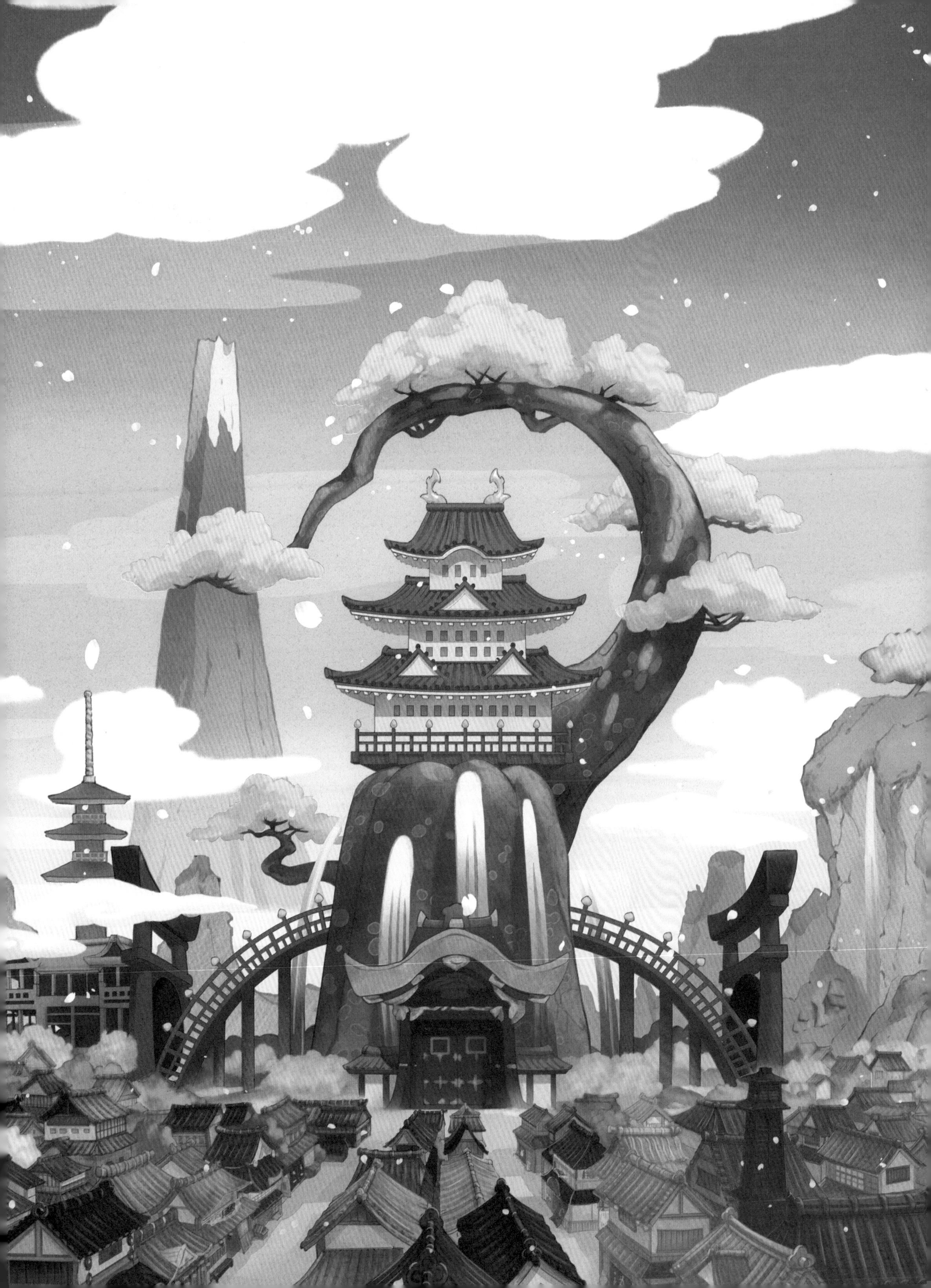

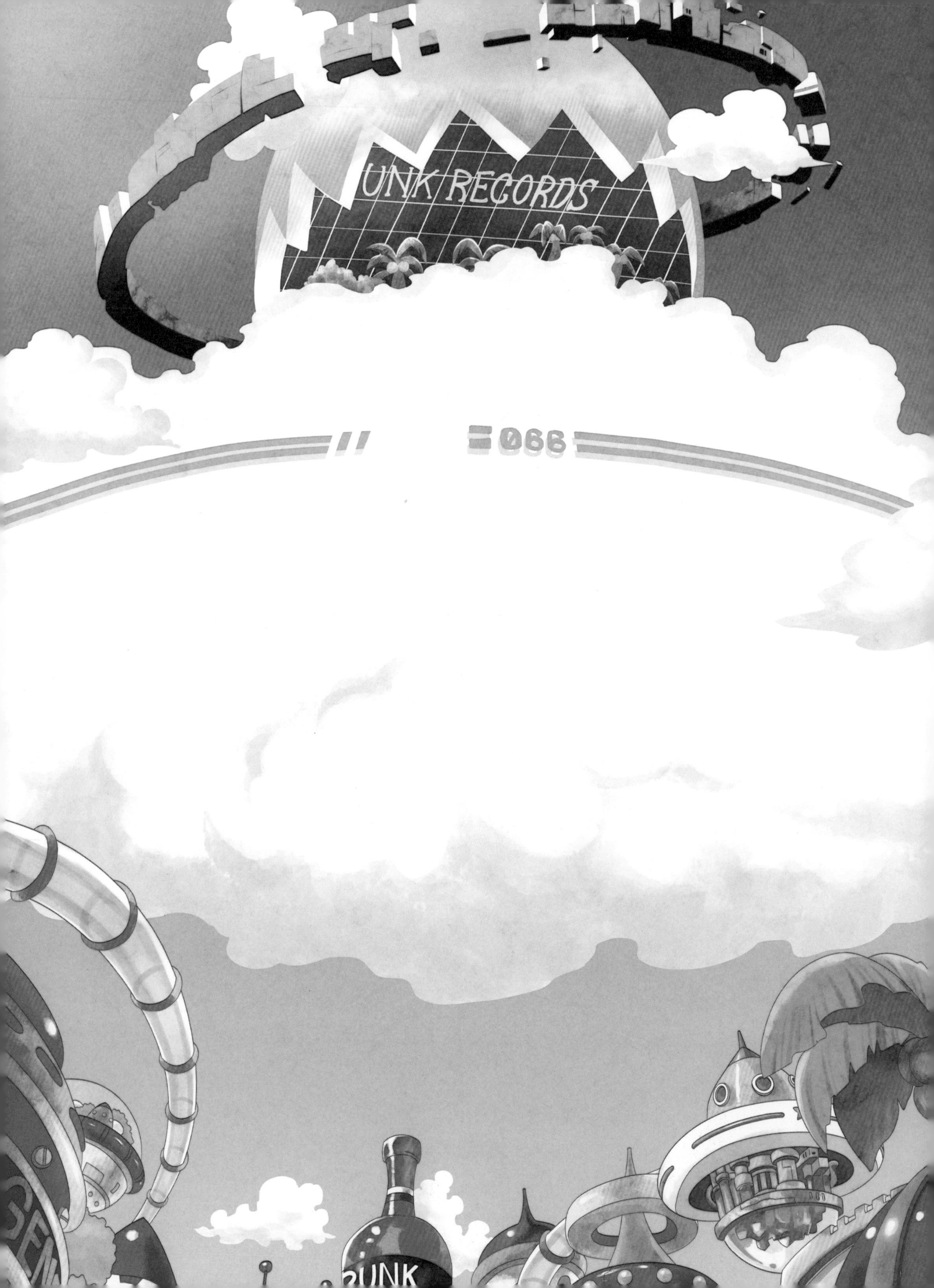
UNK RECORDS
066

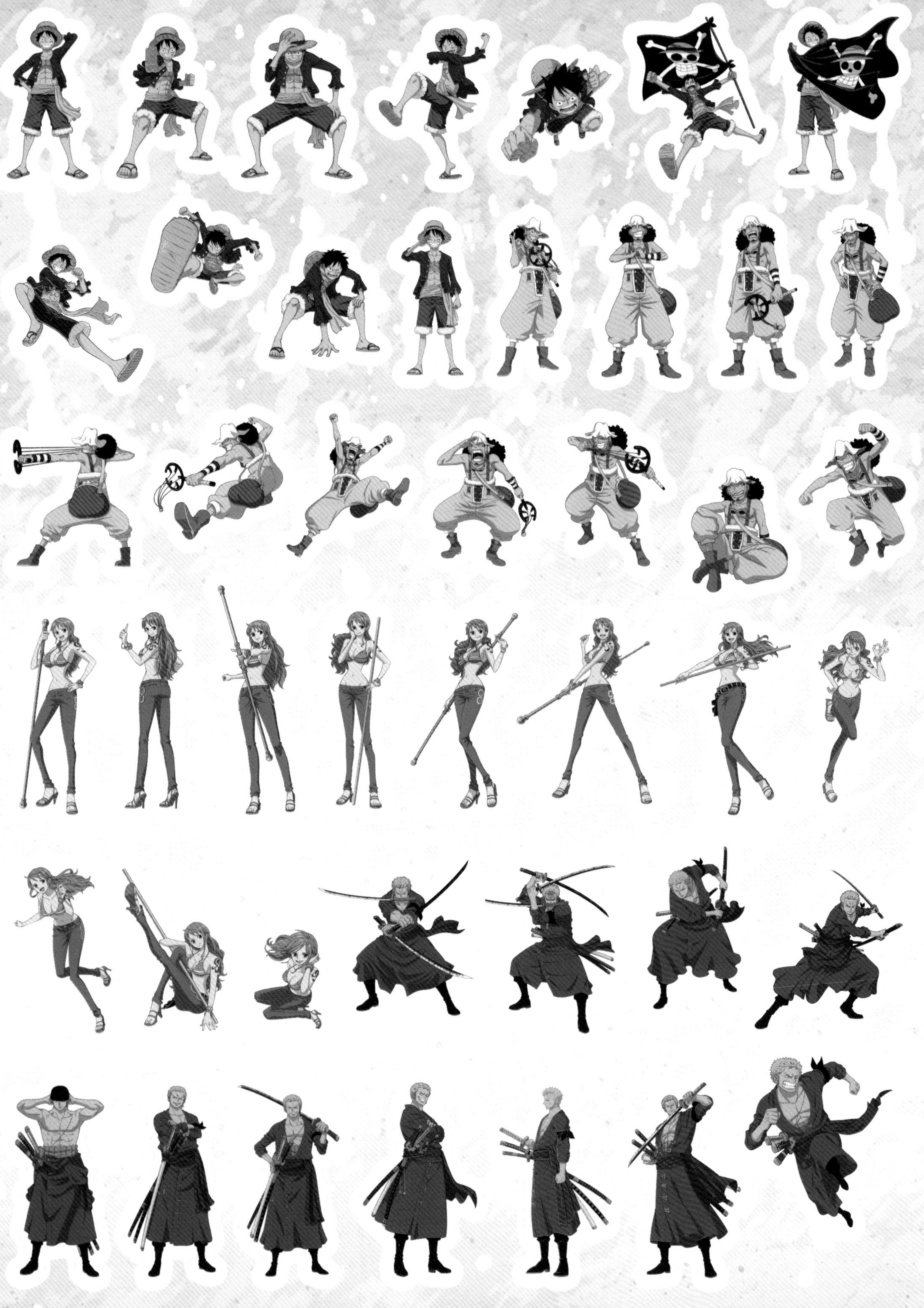

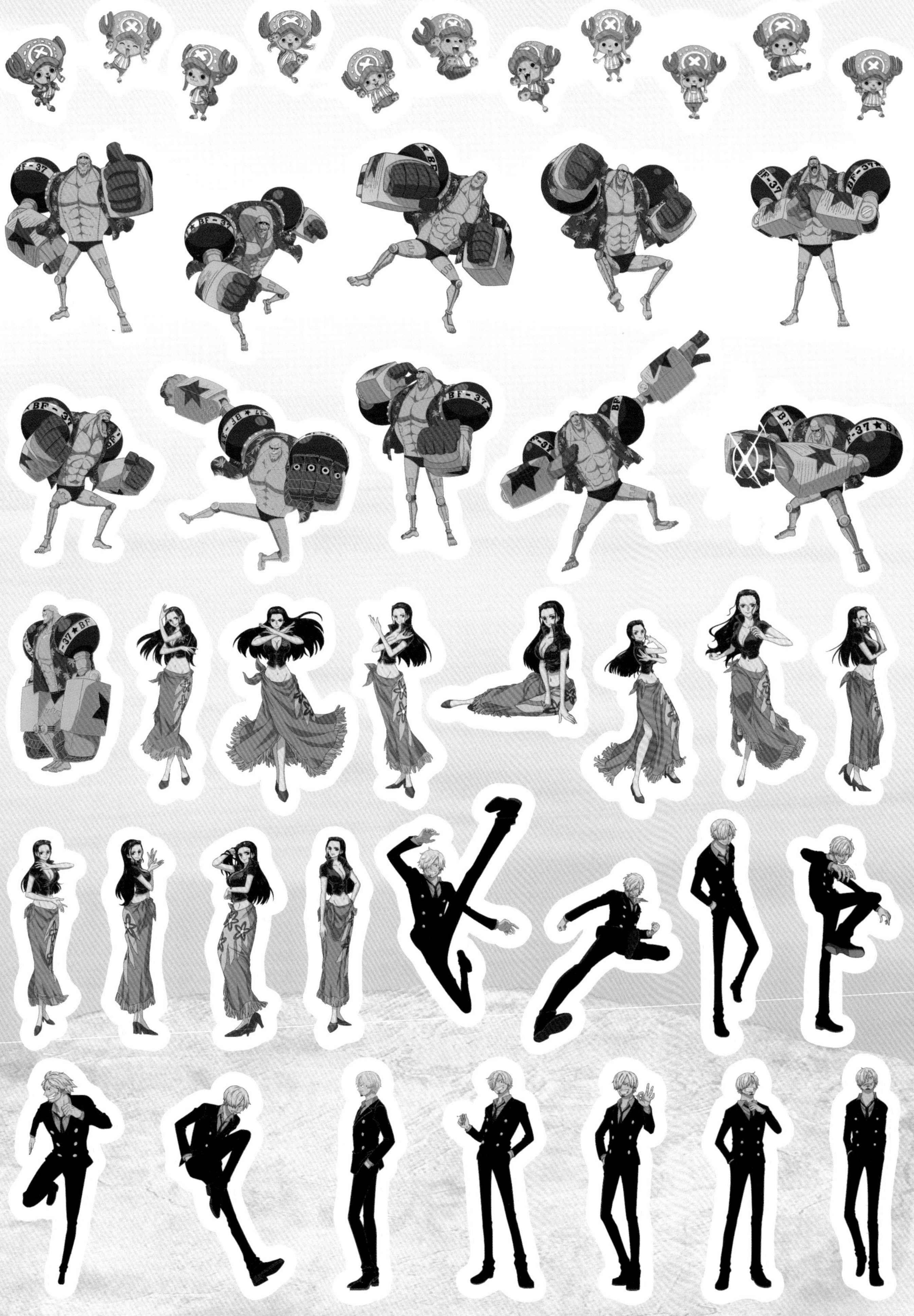

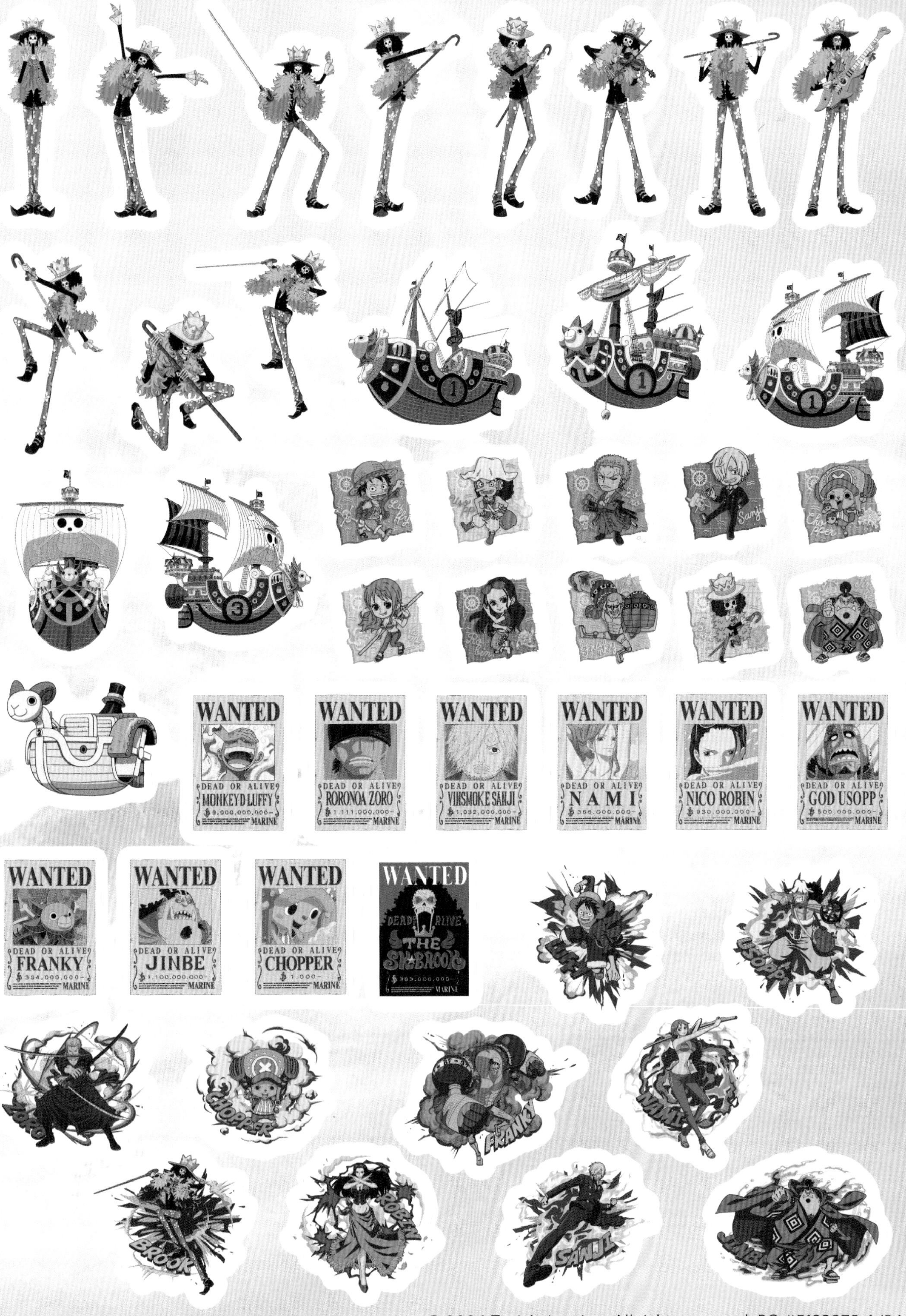
WANTED
DEAD OR ALIVE
MONKEY·D·LUFFY
3,000,000,000–
MARINE
WANTED
DEAD OR ALIVE
RORONOA ZORO
1,111,000,000–
MARINE
WANTED
DEAD OR ALIVE
VINSMOKE SANJI
1,032,000,000–
MARINE
WANTED
DEAD OR ALIVE
NAMI
366,000,000–
MARINE
WANTED
DEAD OR ALIVE
NICO ROBIN
930,000,000–
MARINE
WANTED
DEAD OR ALIVE
GOD USOPP
500,000,000–
MARINE
WANTED
DEAD OR ALIVE
FRANKY
394,000,000–
MARINE
WANTED
DEAD OR ALIVE
JINBE
1,100,000,000–
MARINE
WANTED
DEAD OR ALIVE
CHOPPER
1,000–
MARINE
WANTED
DEAD OR ALIVE
383,000,000–
USOPP
CHOPPER
FRANKY
NAMI
BROOK
ROBIN
SANJI

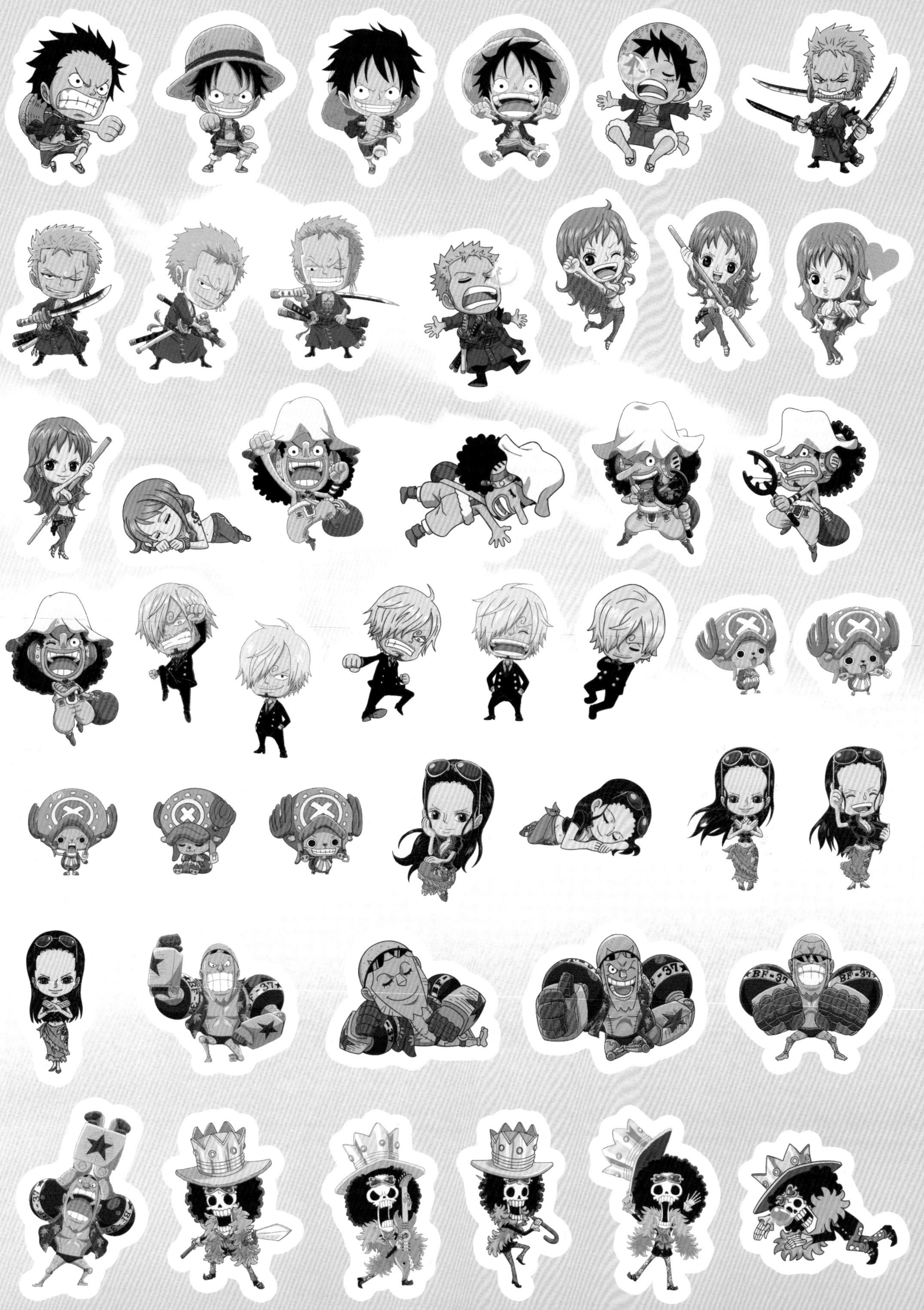

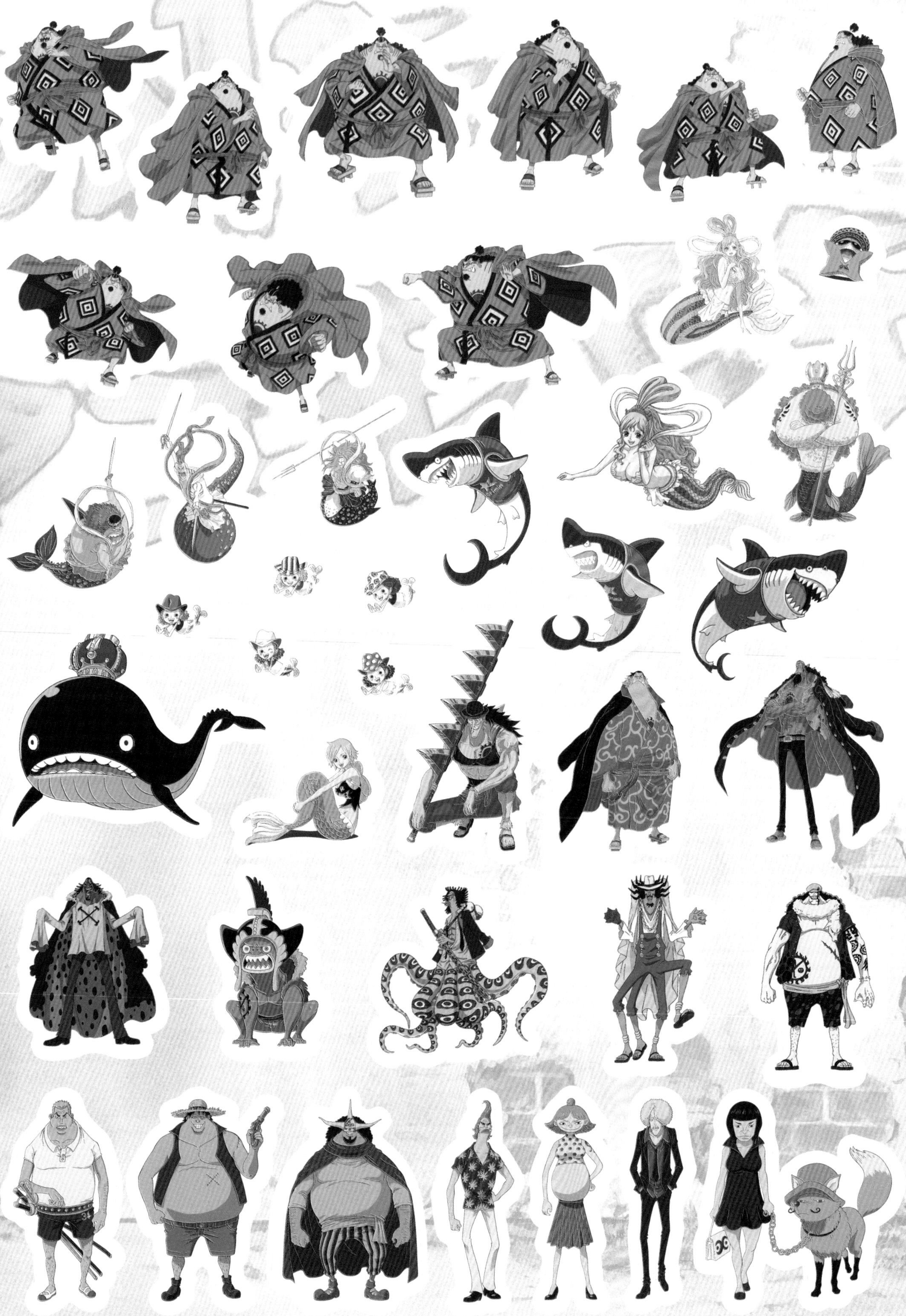

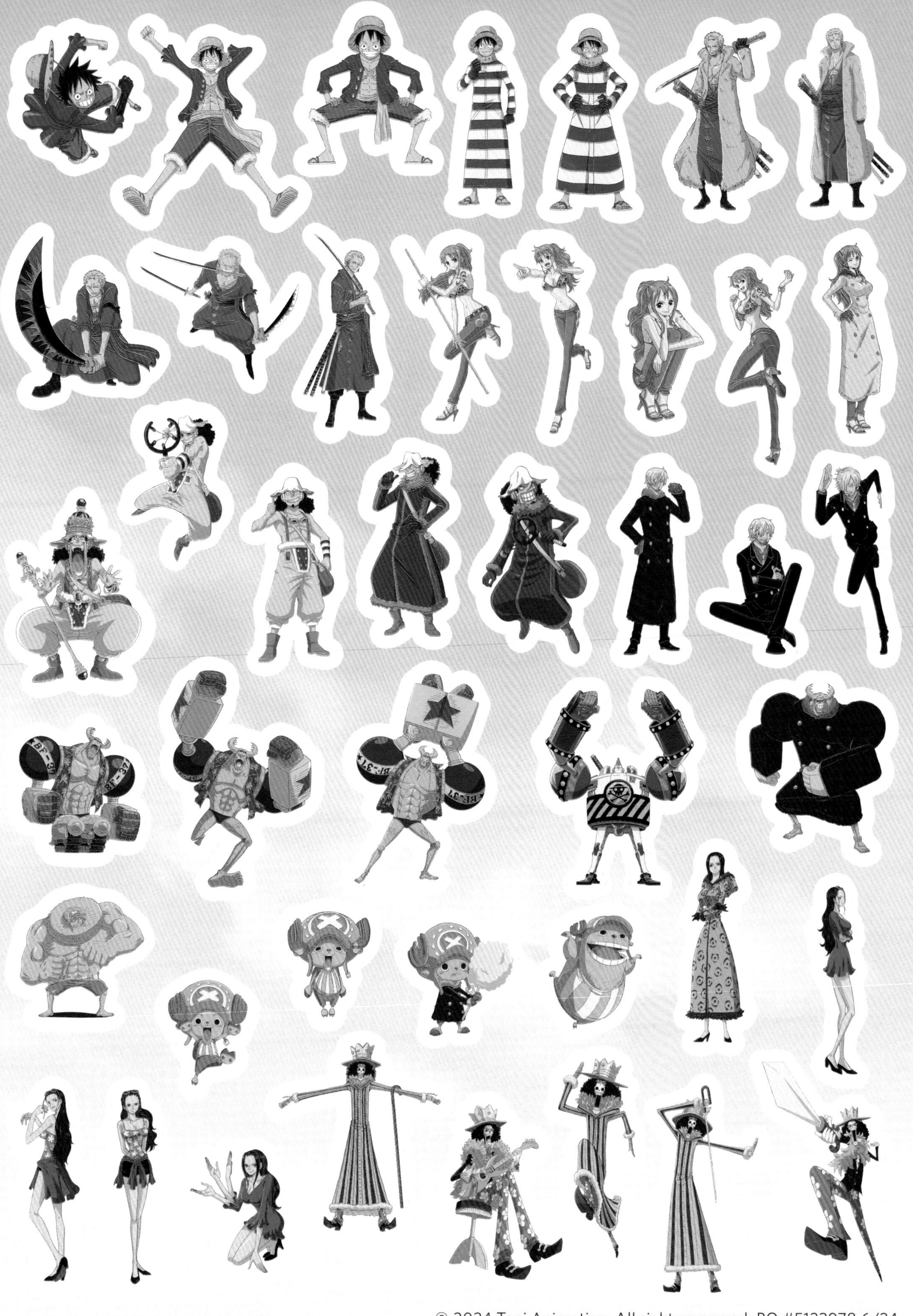

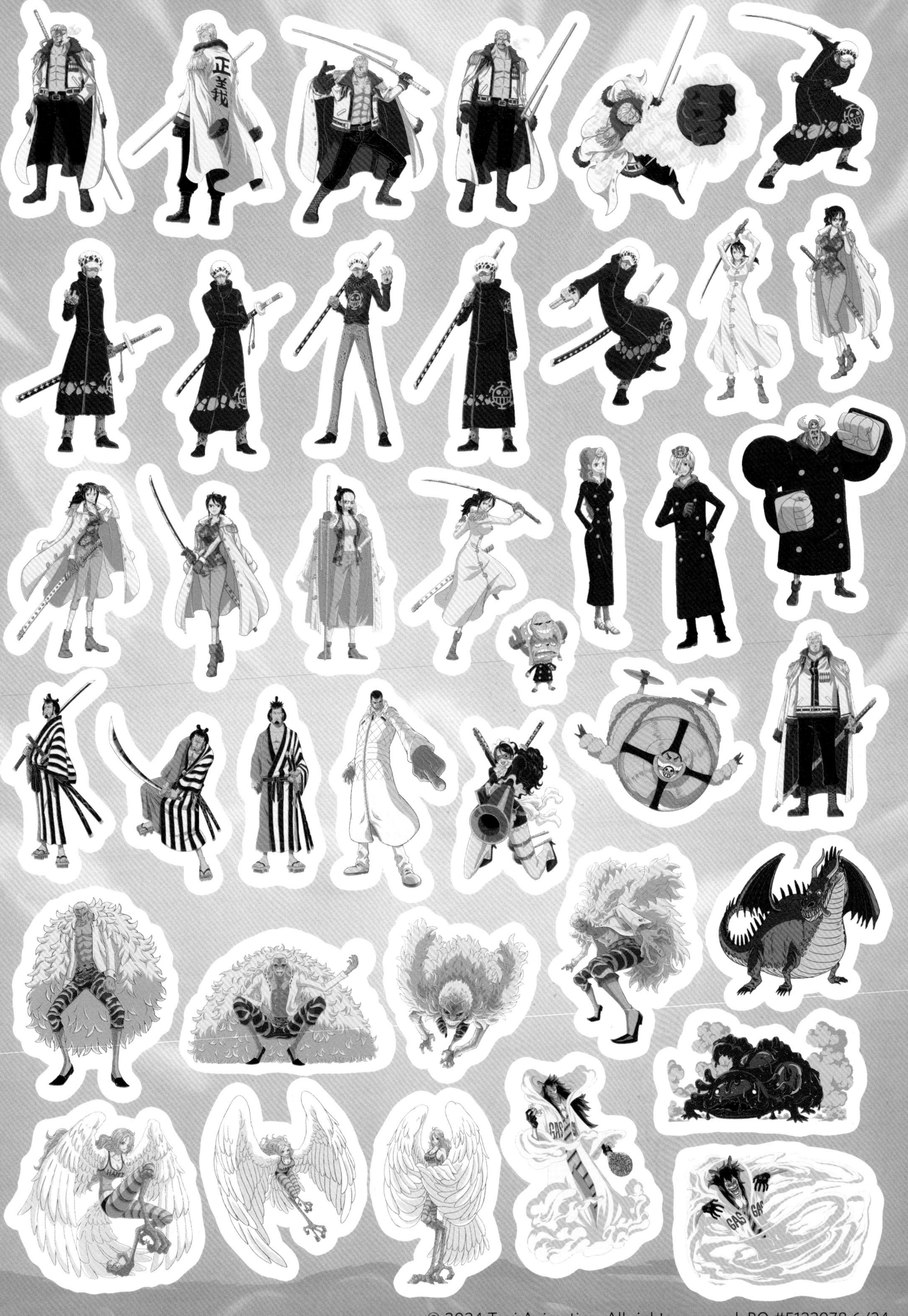
正義
GAS

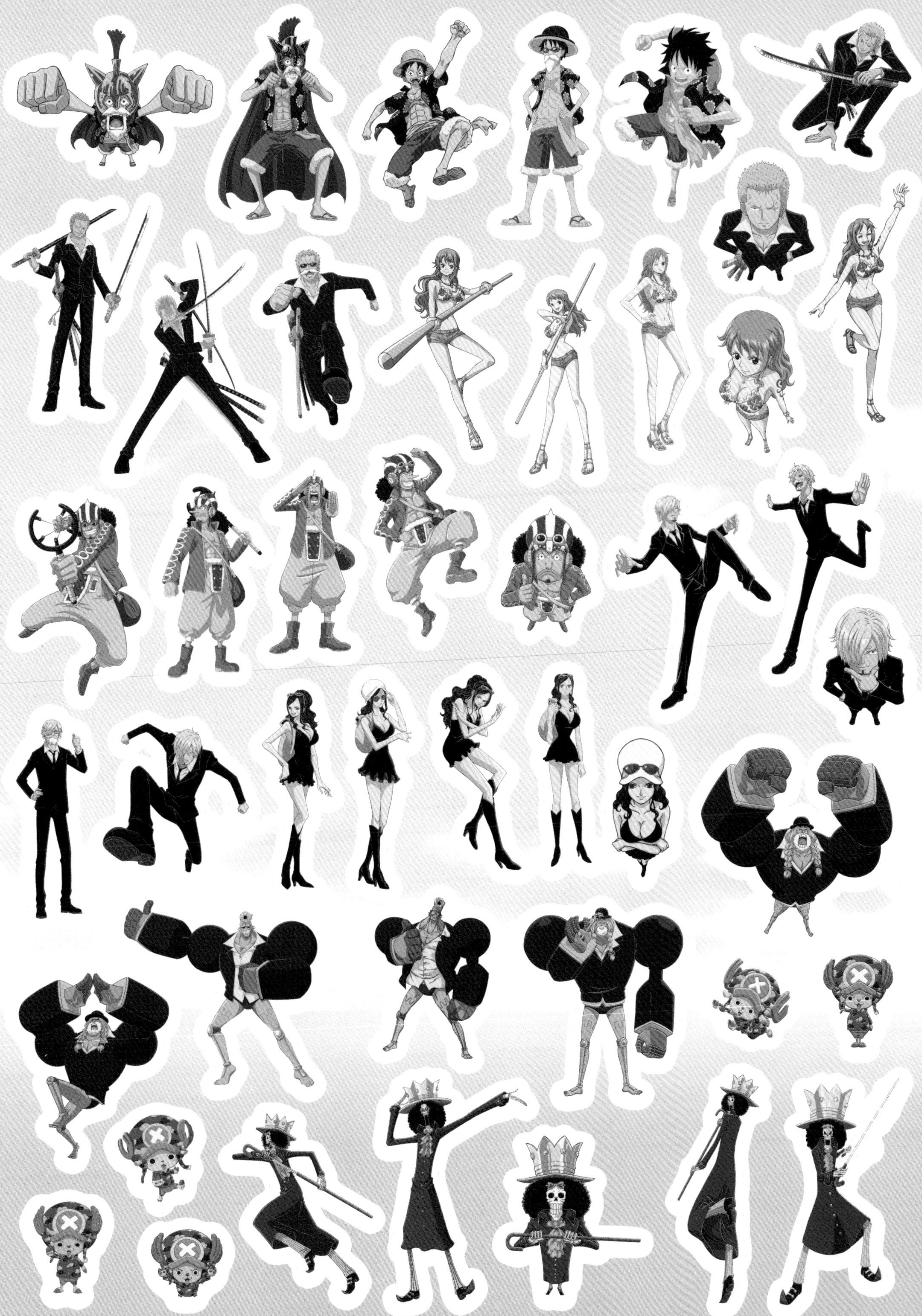

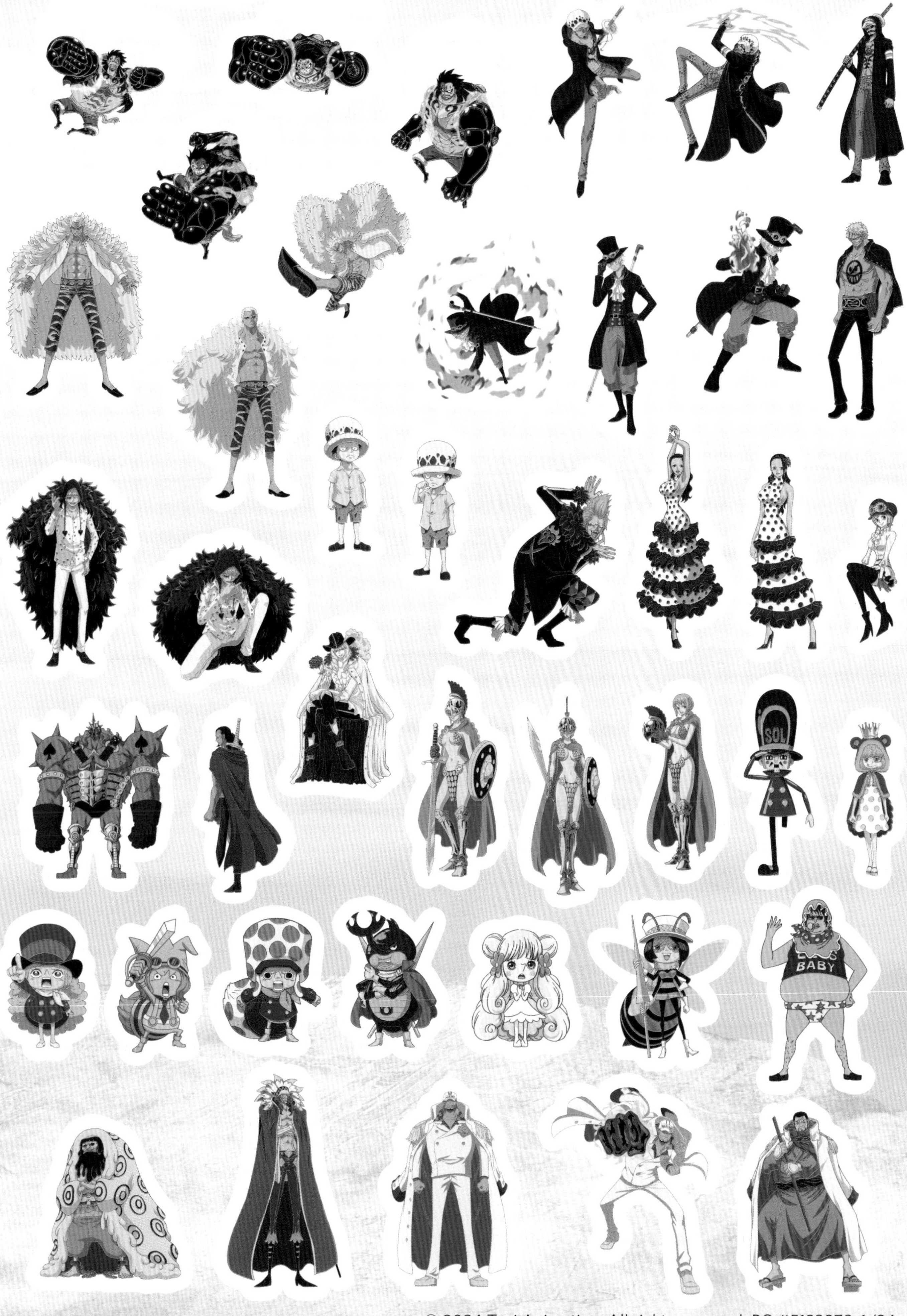
SOL
BABY

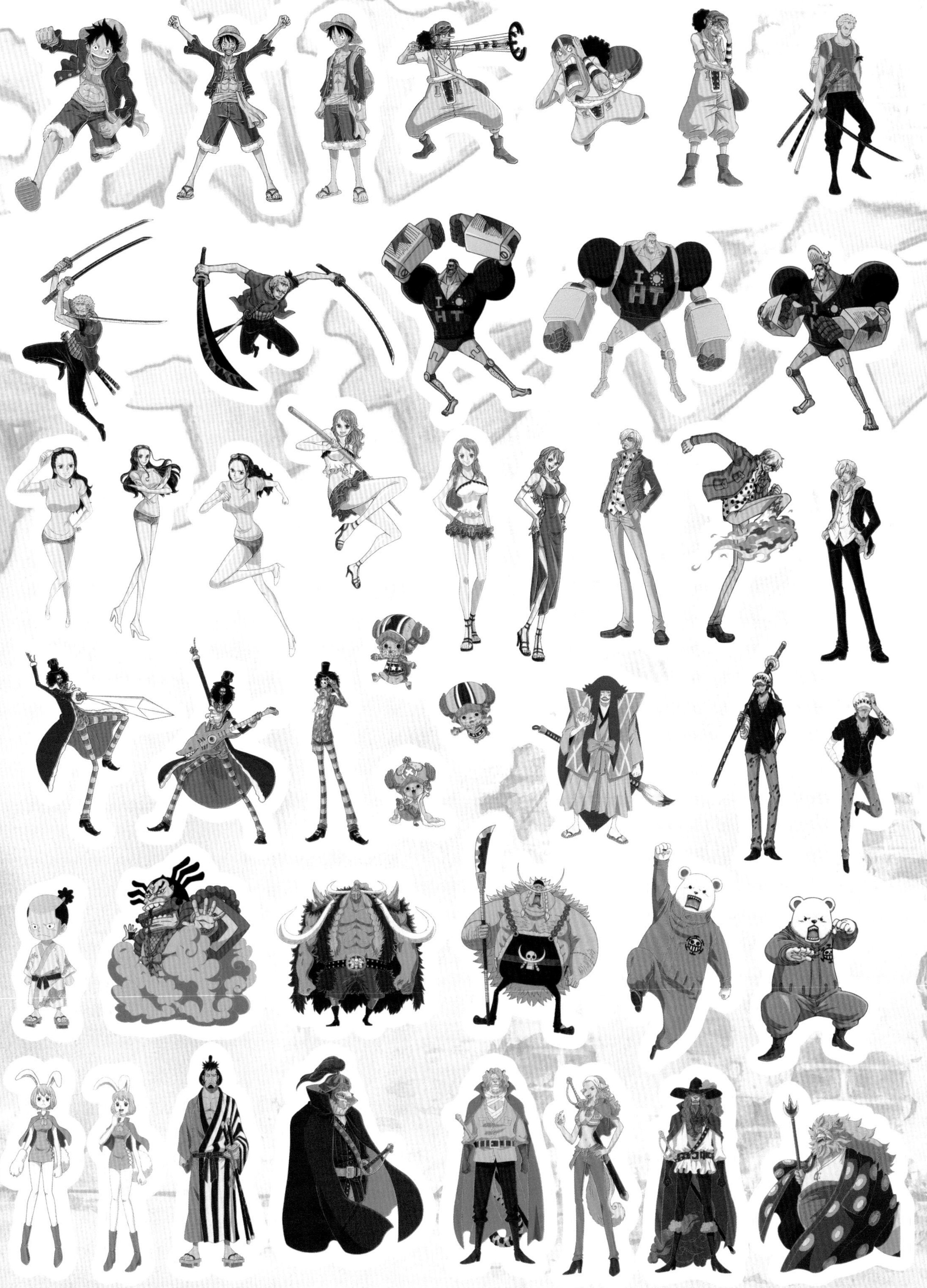

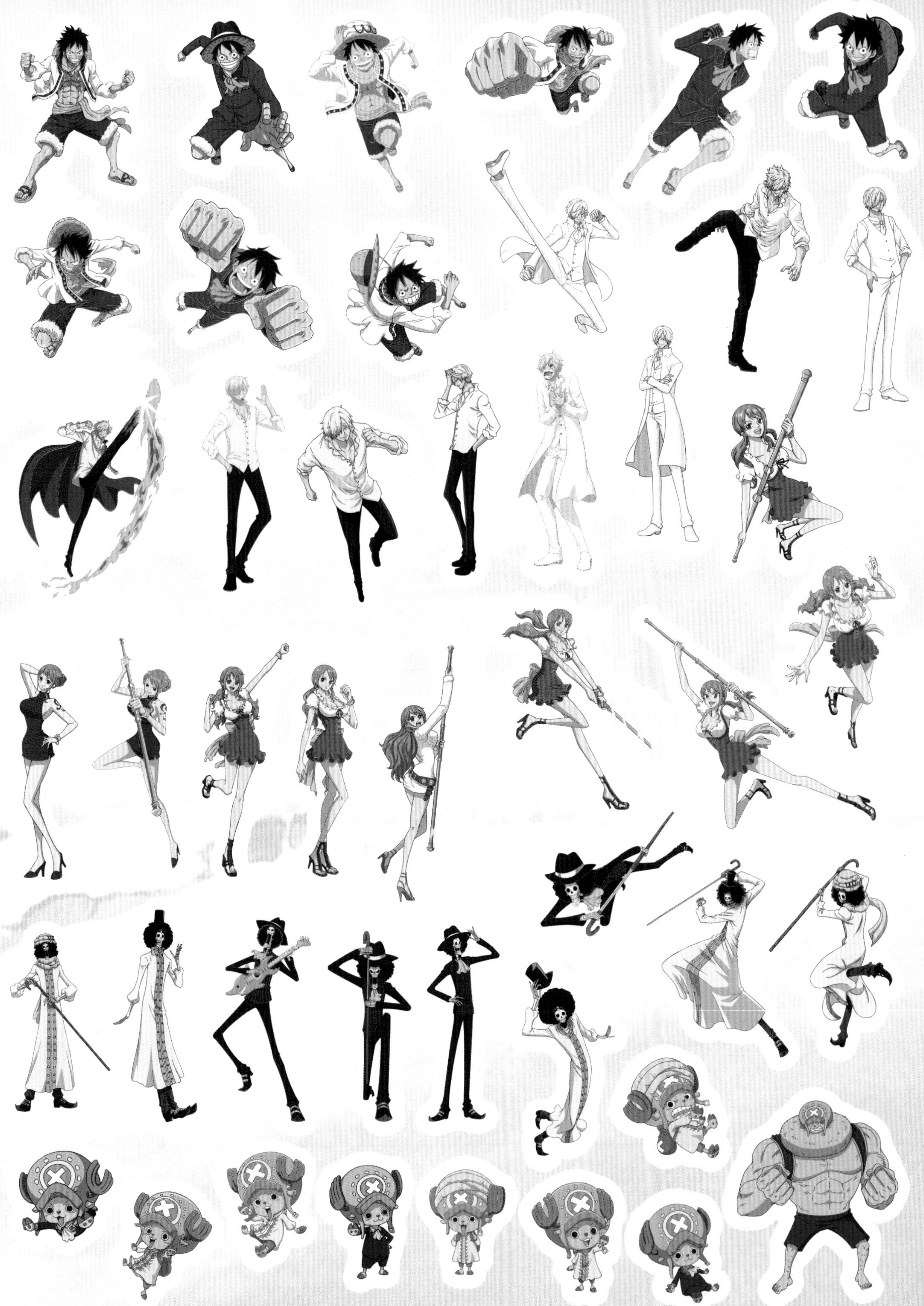

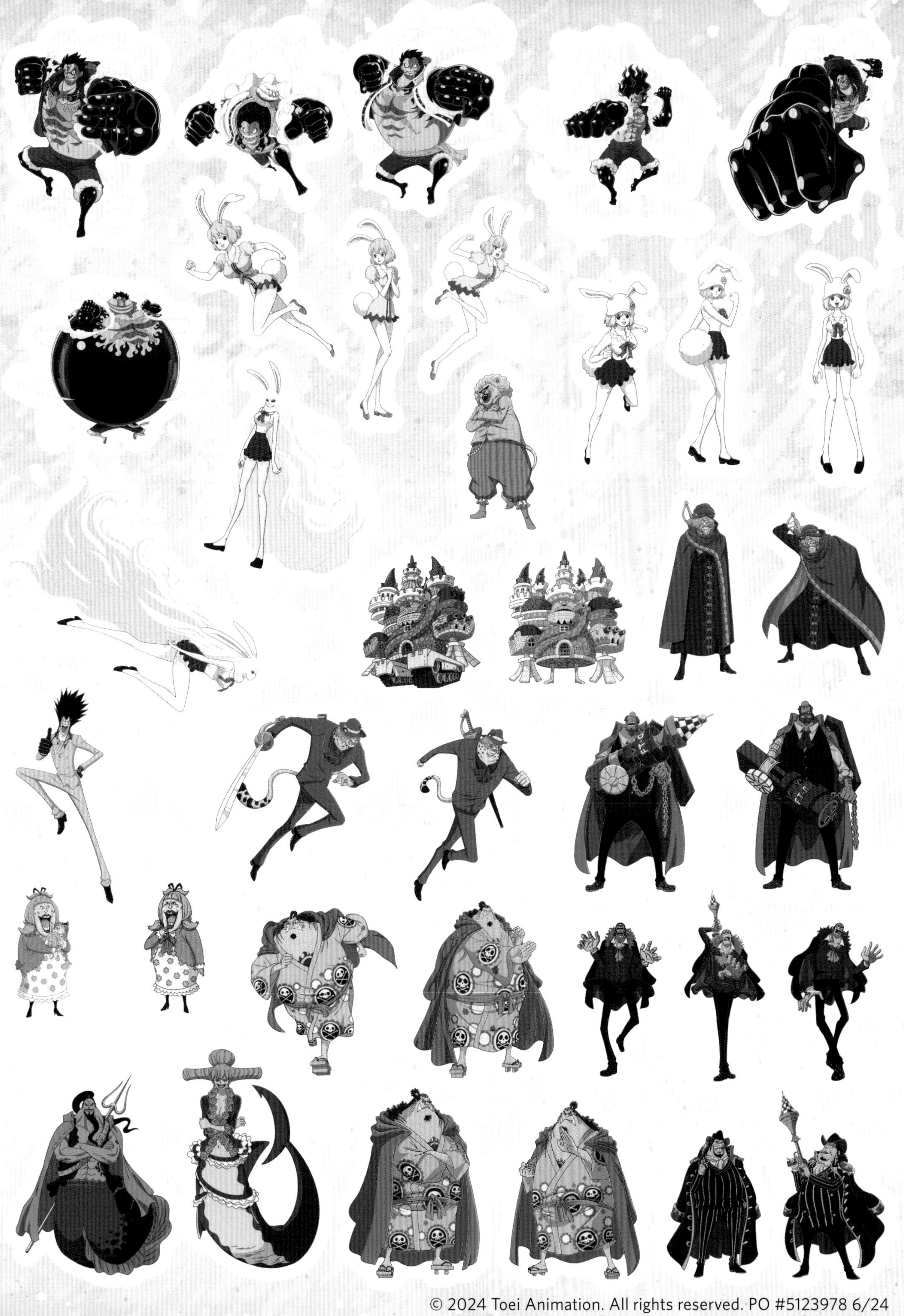

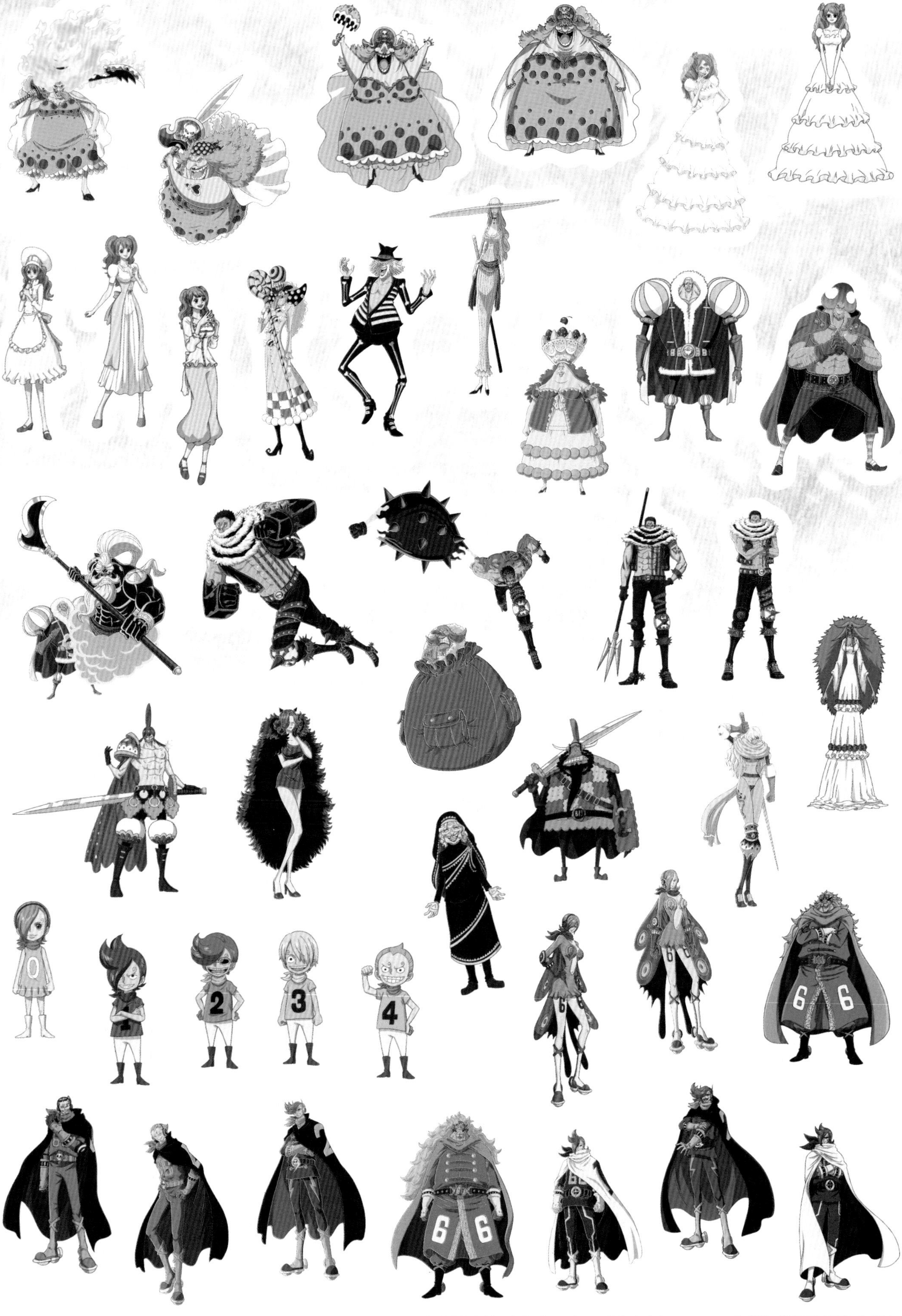

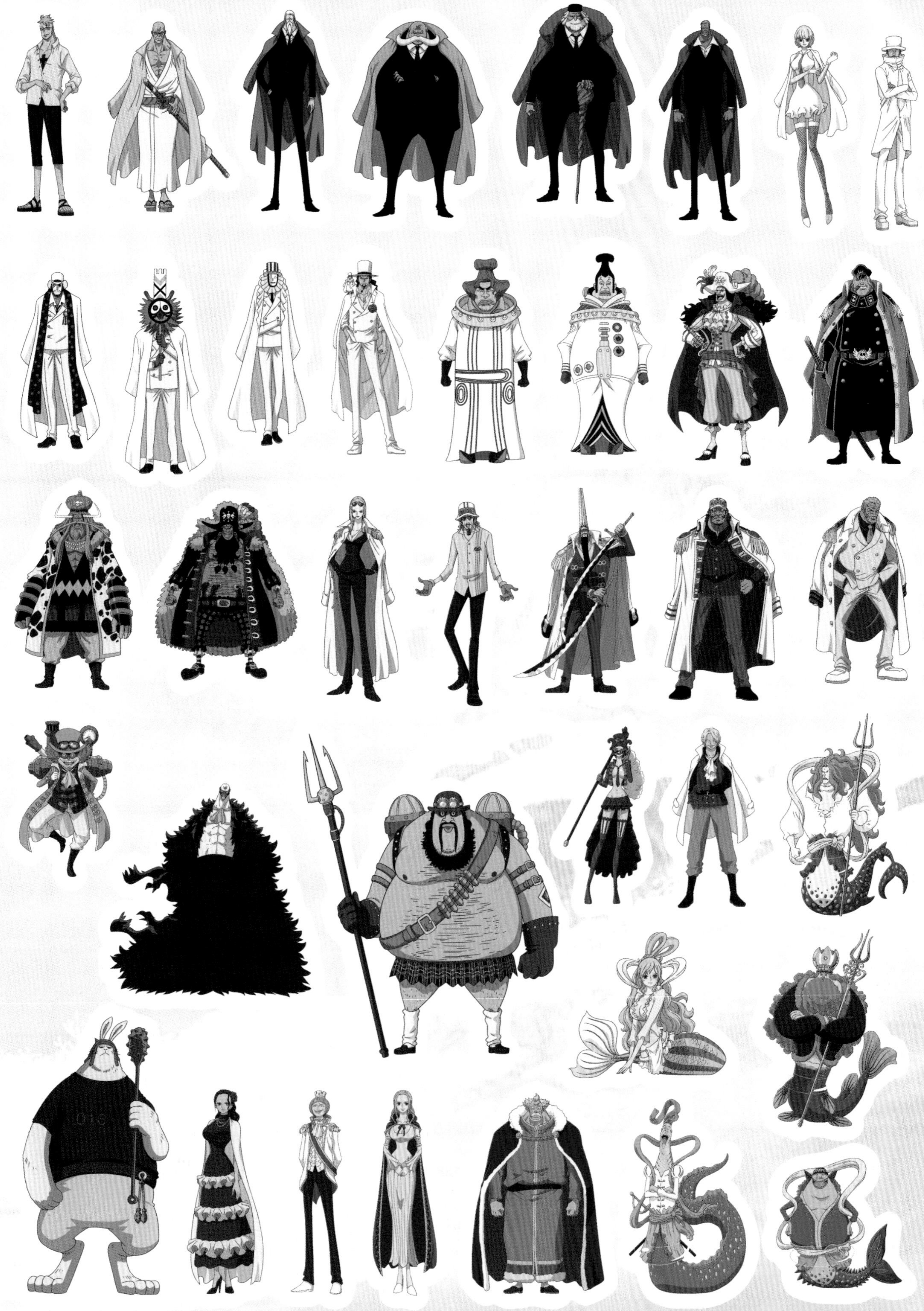

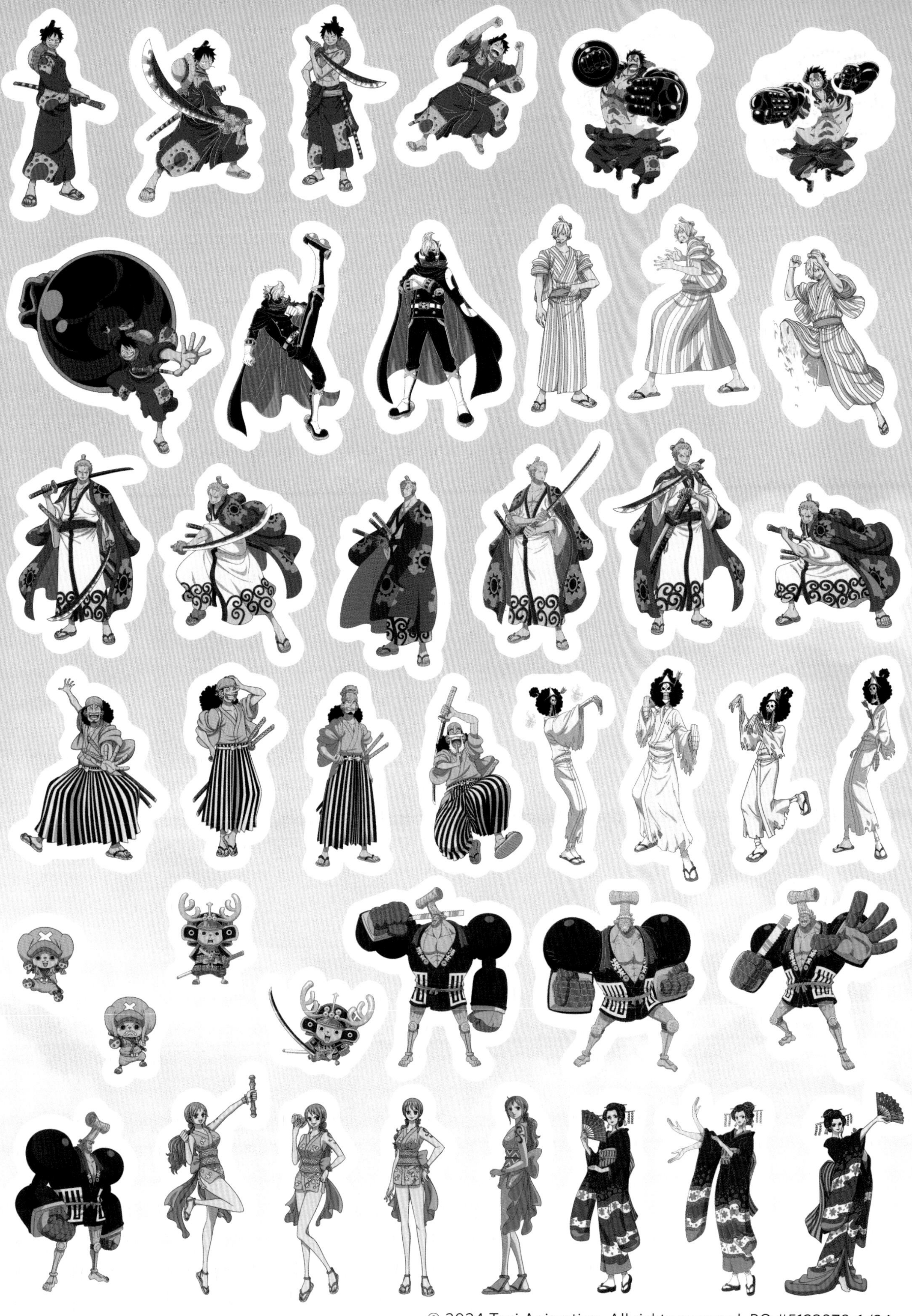

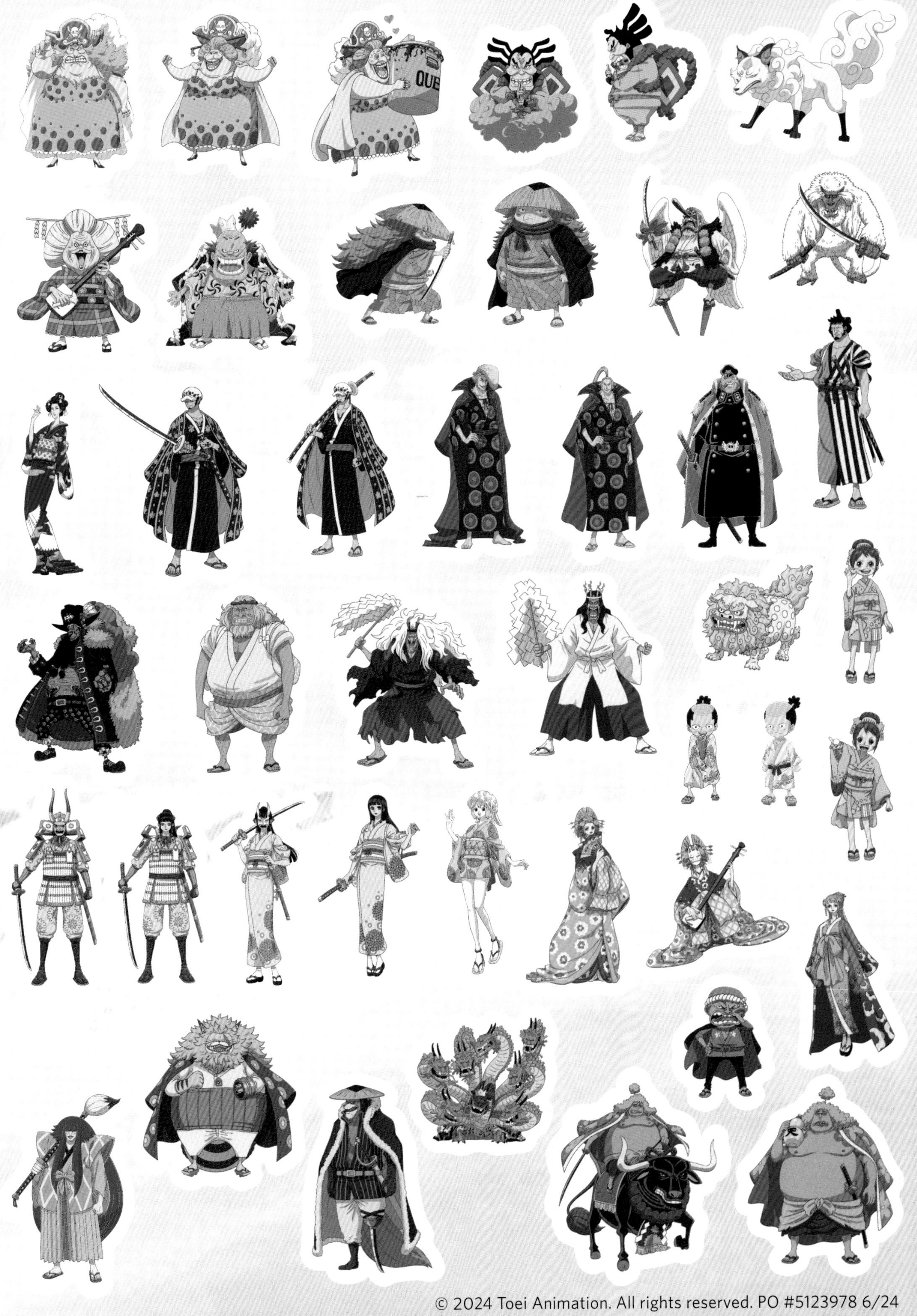
QUE

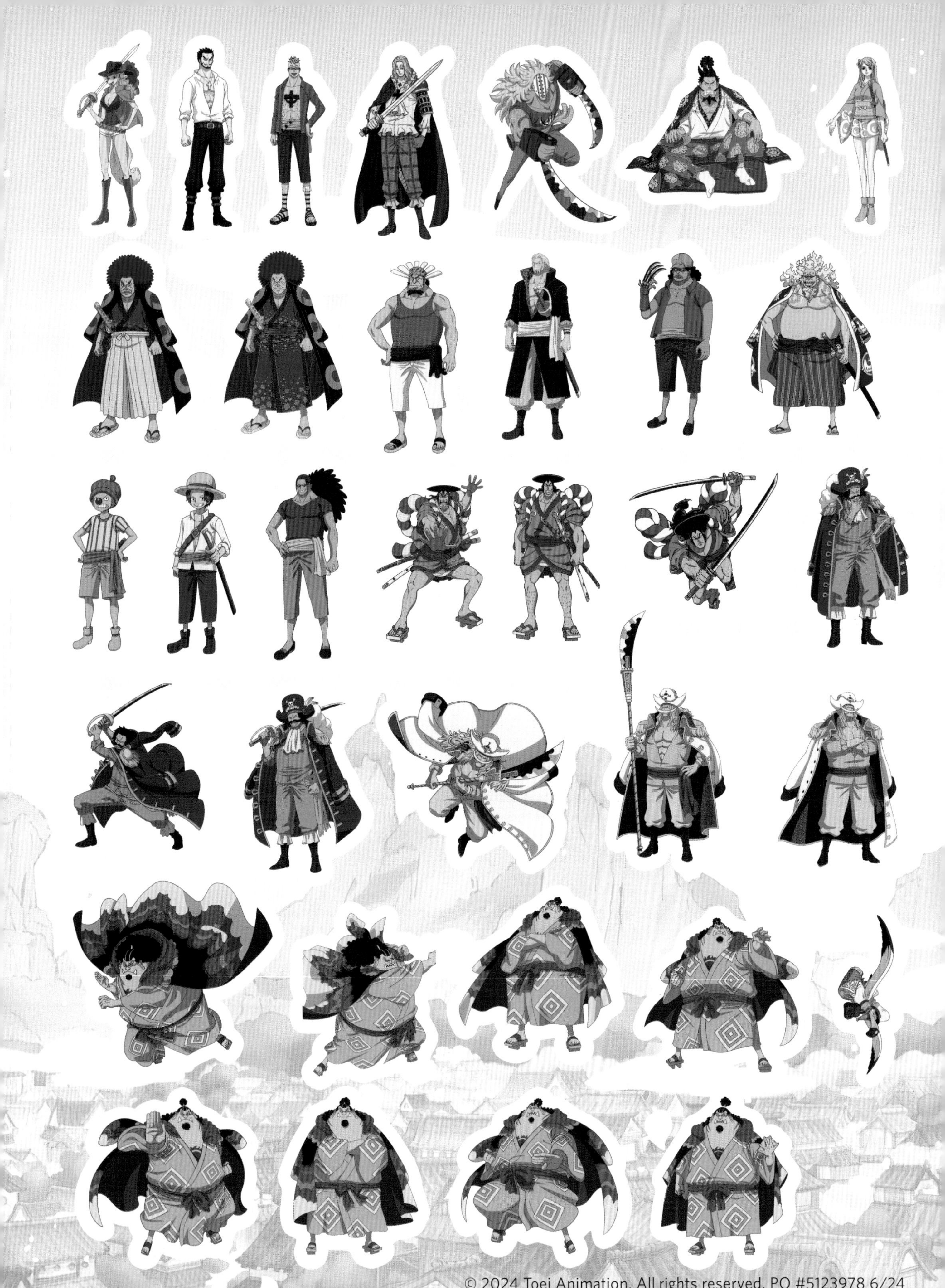

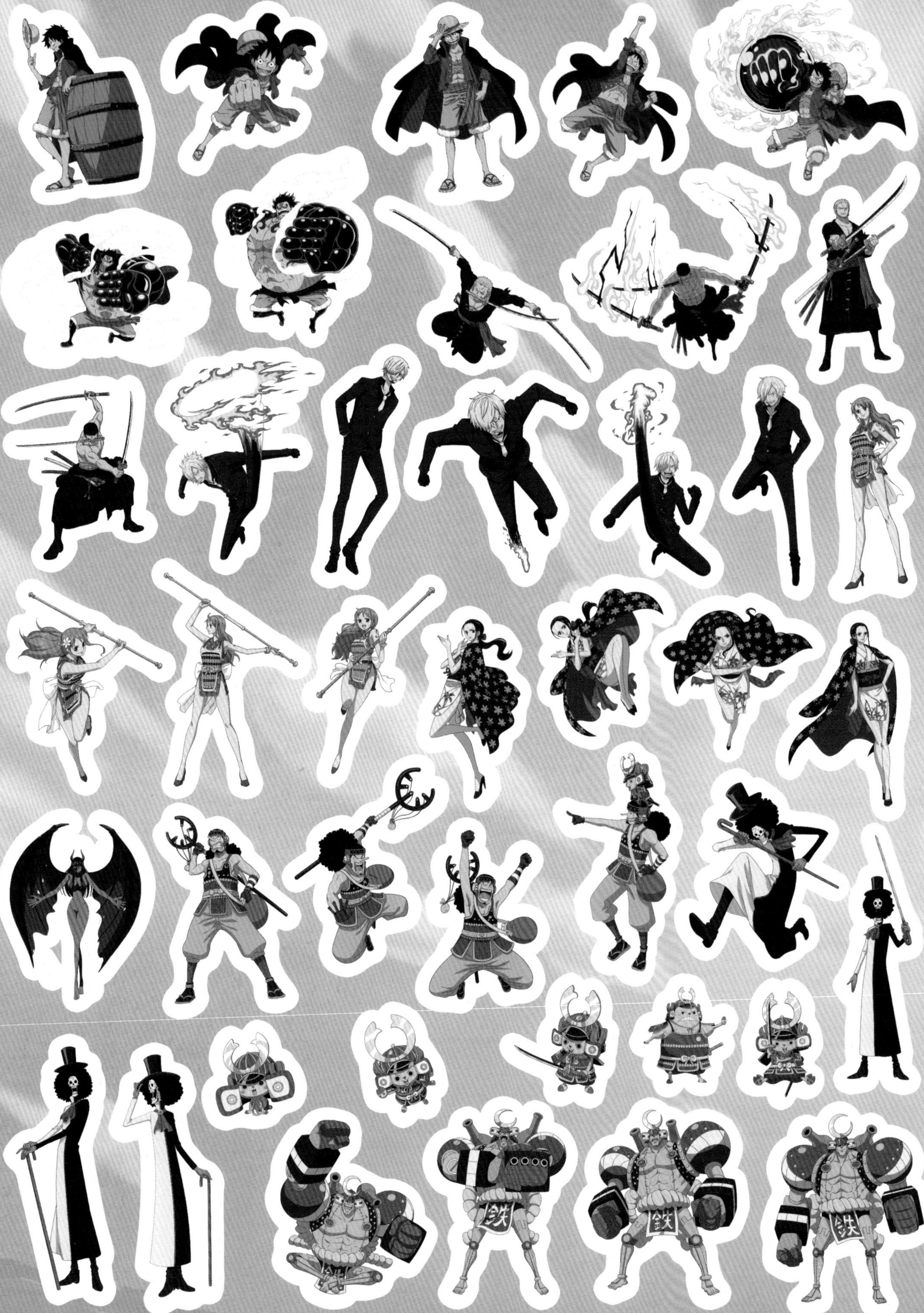

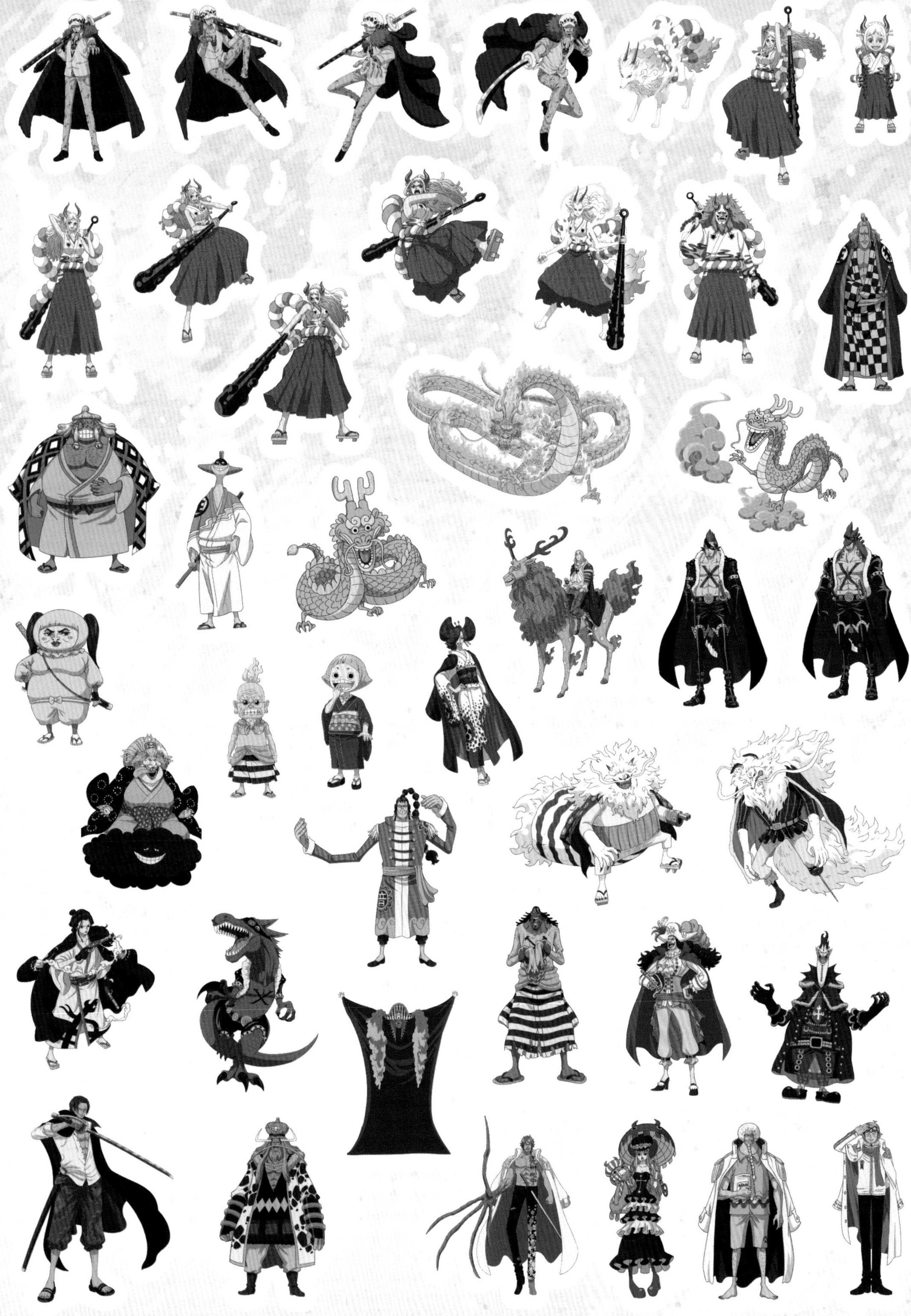

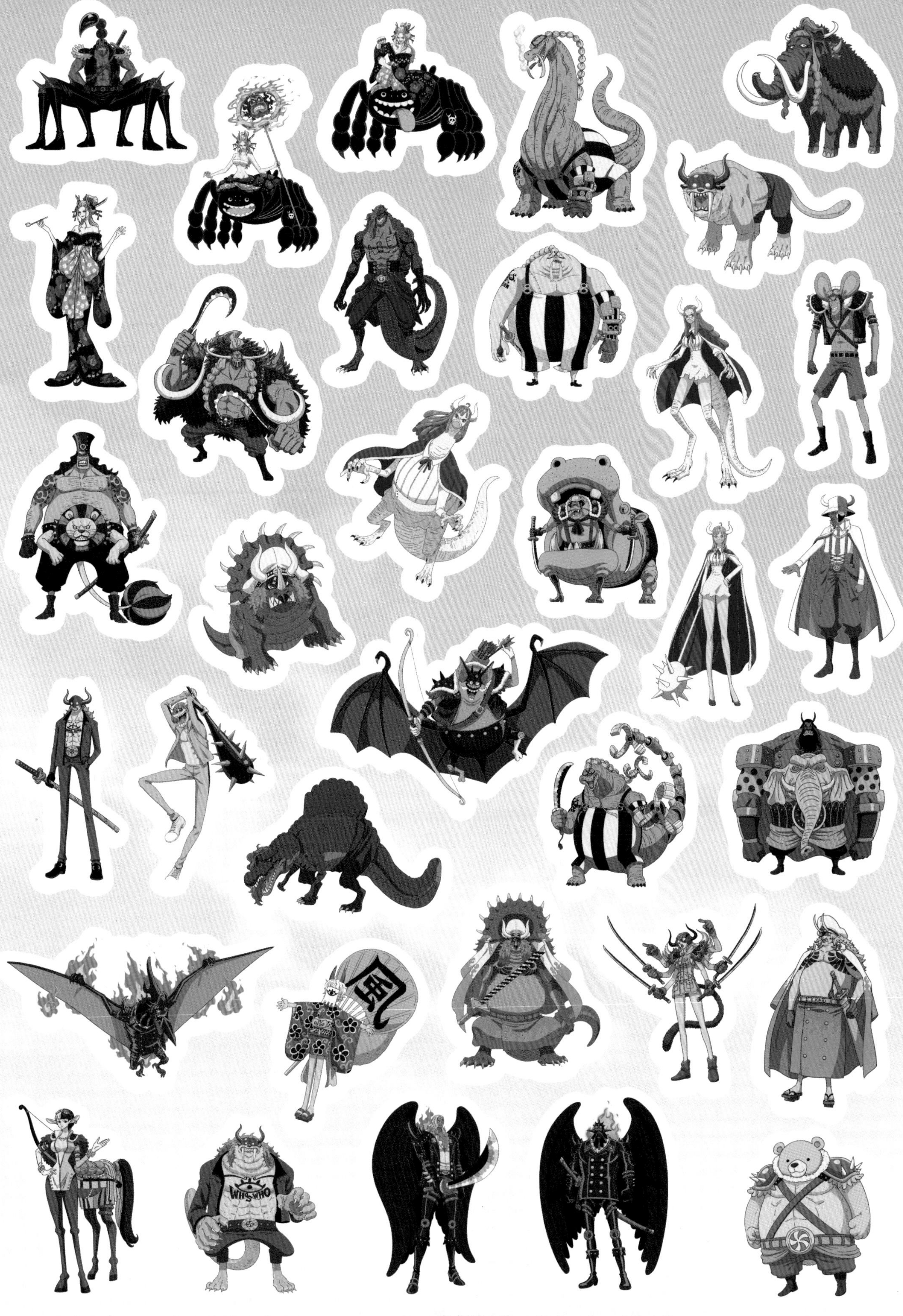

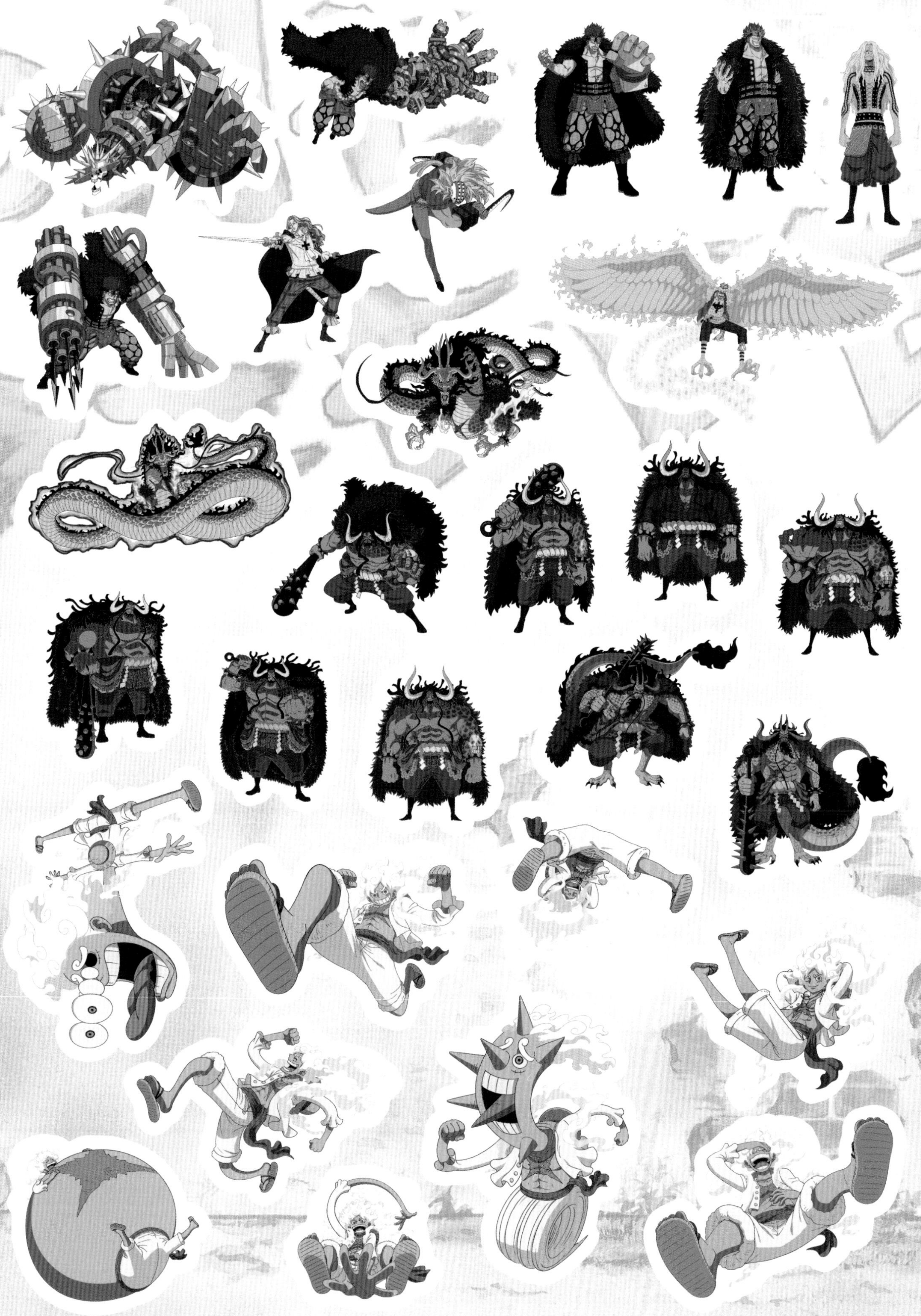

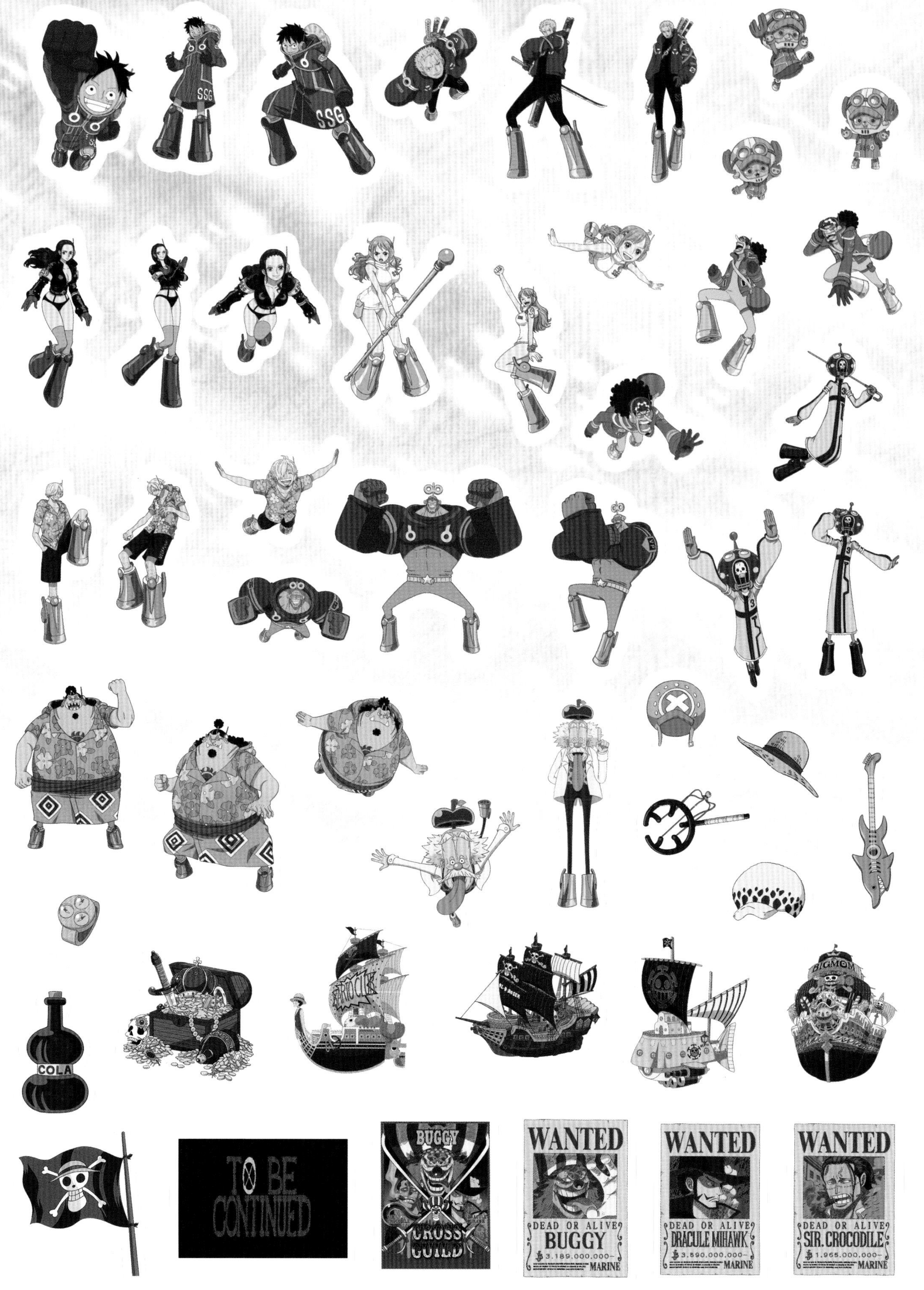
SSG
SSG
COLA
TO BE
CONTINUED
BUGGY
CROSS
GUILD
WANTED
DEAD OR ALIVE
BUGGY
3.189.000.000-
MARINE
WANTED
DEAD OR ALIVE
DRACULE MIHAWK
3.590.000.000-
MARINE
WANTED
DEAD OR ALIVE
SIR. CROCODILE
1.965.000.000-
MARINE

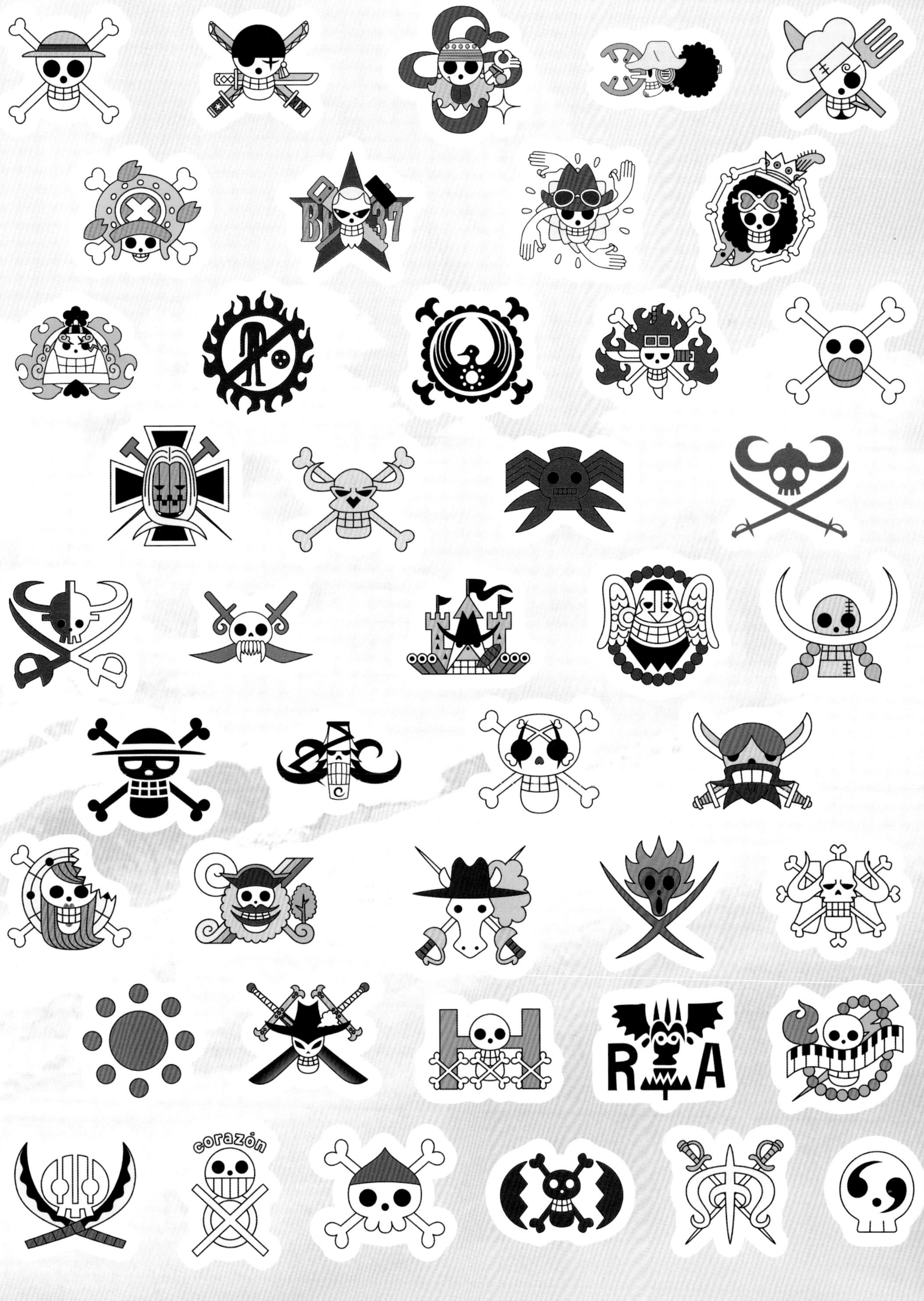
corazón

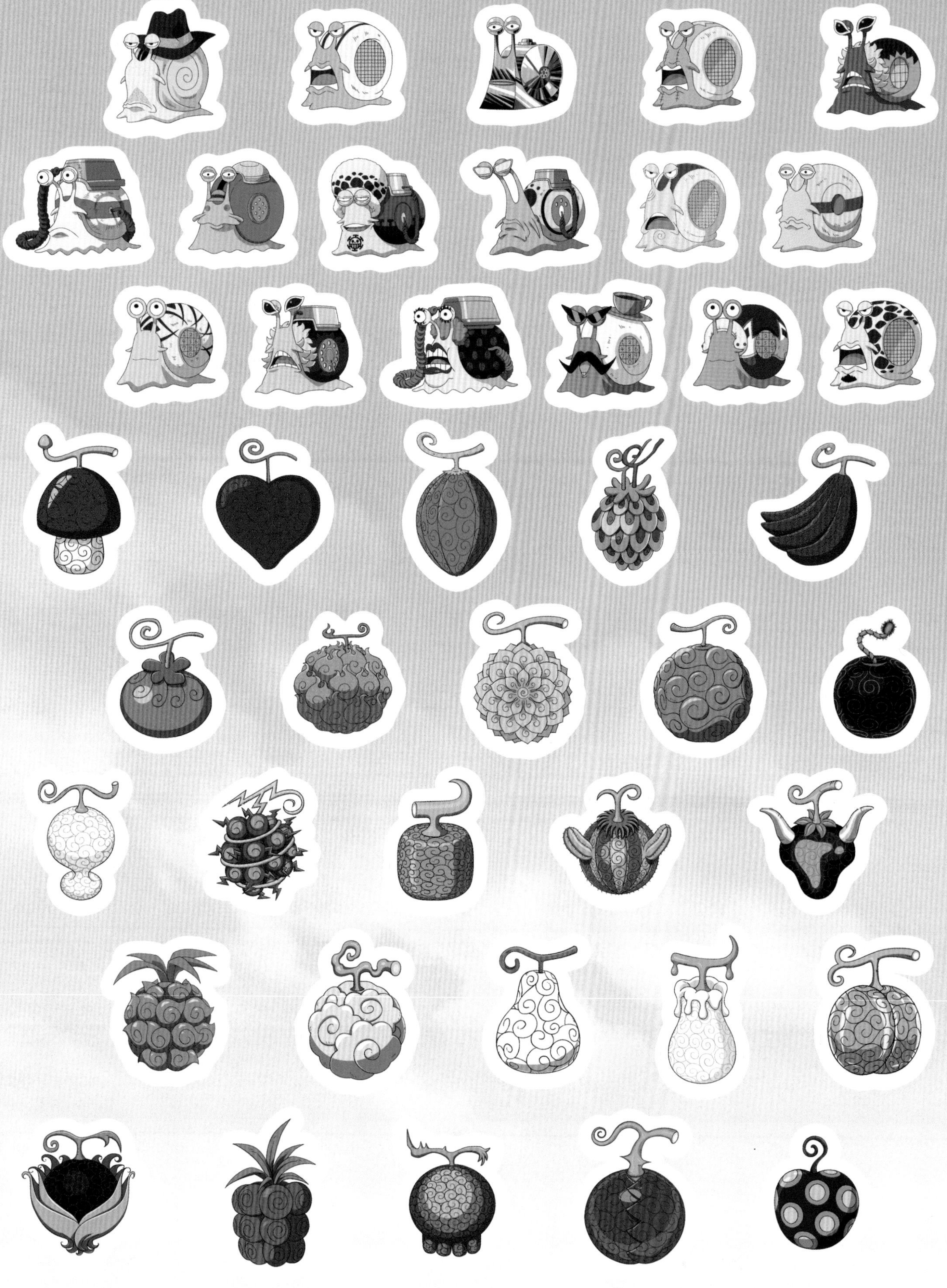

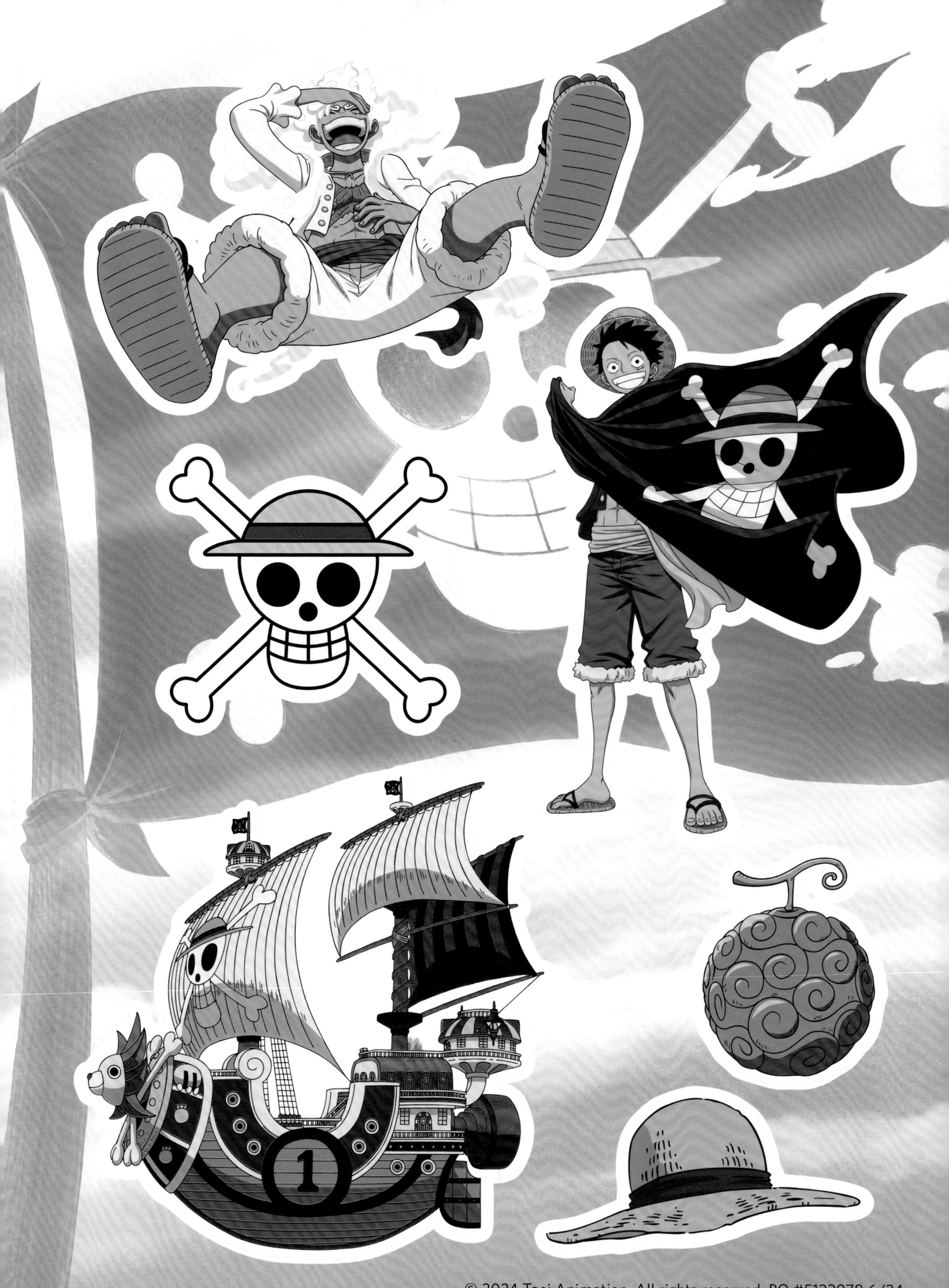
1